Sylvie's Riddle

Sylvie's Riddle

ALAN WALL

QUARTET BOOKS

First published in 2008 by
Quartet Books Limited
A member of the Namara Group
27 Goodge Street, London W1T 2LD

A catalogue record for this book
is available from the British Library

ISBN   978 0 7043 7134 7

Typeset by Antony Gray

Printed and bound in Great Britain by
T J International Ltd, Padstow, Cornwall

NOTE

In 2003 I was awarded an Arts Council/AHRB Fellowship to work for a year with the particle physicist Goronwy Tudor Jones of the School of Physics and Astronomy at Birmingham University. The aim of the Fellowship was to promote understanding between the arts and sciences. The collaboration proved fruitful. It continues to result in new work. We have already published various essays together, such as 'Extremities of Perception' (*Leonardo*). This novel is the first book-length result of that fertile year. I am greatly indebted to the Arts Council of Great Britain and the AHRB. It would be hard to express my gratitude to Goronwy Tudor Jones himself, whose gift for exposition let me catch a glimpse of the astonishing insights of modern physics. This book is dedicated to him.

I am also indebted to the Royal Literary Fund for RLF Fellowships at Warwick University and Liverpool John Moores.

Contents

To

GORONWY TUDOR JONES

If this should be written on the mind, then always in a fugitive ink . . .

FRIEDRICH EULAND

Mystery Play

The man finds enough money in his greatcoat pocket, once deep blue but now greying with age, to buy a coffee. Only as he sits down to drink the coffee does it occur to him that he has no idea where the money came from. Nor for that matter the greatcoat. And where did he come from?

He drinks the coffee. Although he remembers the word *coffee* he has no knowledge of the taste. A taste of hotness, gushing down a drainpipe. He fumbles through the pockets of the unknown coat. There is a card. He takes it out. An oblong piece of plastic, blue and red. A library card. The name is written in black ink: Owen Treadle. He drinks more of the coffee; now he can taste only scalding milk. A cow's udder dunked in a cauldron. He rises from the formica table, stained with ten thousand cheap meals and as many cigarette butts, and walks across to the counter. The woman behind it in her sky-blue overall stares at him without interest.

'Do you know Owen Treadle?' he says.

'Owen Treadle.' She repeats the name slowly, non-committally. Her blonde hair is permed. The perplexity in her eyes is magnified by her thick glasses. He sees a shoal of tiny fishes in a bottle, the subaquean thrash of cold silver flesh. 'Owen Treadle. Rings a bell.'

'Do I look like him?'

'What?'

'Do I ring a bell? Do I ring the same bell the name just rang?

Do you think I might be Owen Treadle?' Where all these words were coming from, he had no idea.

'Well, I'd have thought if anyone should know that it would have been you, darling. Wouldn't you say? Are you going back to the hostel?'

'The hostel.'

'St Clare's, my love. I think that's where you normally come from, isn't it, when you come at all? But you've never told me your name, all the different times you've been here.'

Outside he stopped the first person he met.

'Could you tell me the way to St Clare's?' The old man, bent but cheerful, had a plastic bag in his hand, swollen with potatoes and a cauliflower. The man in the greatcoat looked from the cauliflower to the little old man's head; one was shinier and smoother. That was the one you mustn't boil. He remembered.

'Carry on along that road until you come to the bridge over the canal, and it's opposite the steam mill.' He heard a piston from another century shrieking in spite and potency. Heard pitmen in thin seams, wheezing with emphysema. Heard the sound of history begrimed. Was that where he had to go back to then? Back into the filth of history?

He found Saint Clare's with no trouble. In fact, once he had started walking towards it he realised he hadn't needed any directions in the first place. The streets around him seemed to hold their own information, and now they were sharing it with him. Once inside its door, past the glass window on the left where the uniformed man nodded him through, he knew where to go. He walked up the steps to the second floor, and then along the corridor, pale green paint all around, tropical vegetation gone milky and anaemic, till he came to Room 212. Inside, Alfred was sitting as usual on one of the beds, a leather-bound copy of the Bible open on his lap.

'Hello Owen,' he said. 'The flies on his face are only there because they want to be. Did you hear the buzz of the traffic outside?'

Owen sat on the other bed without taking off his greatcoat. He stared at the much smaller and older man. A goatee beard, yellow and stained. He should wash that. His head largely barren but with a scrubland of whitish hairs straggling on either side. Bright blue eyes. No glasses though, even though he was reading. Unusual that. Blue eyes are often the weakest.

'Have you started remembering anything yet, Owen? You've already been here two days. You normally start to remember by now.'

'What should I remember, Alfred?'

'I'm not telling you. It changes every time. Each year I learn something different. Each year you come, that is. So I'm not telling you.'

Later they sat next to one another in the refectory. Neither of them joined in as the Christian soldiers were exhorted onwards, and their colleagues sang about what a friend they had in Jesus. They ate. Owen found smells, tastes, sensations on his gums and tongue, and tried to slide them into the silk pockets in his mind, or let them swish smoothly through the interstices. They left when the meal was over. Alfred whispered quietly to him: 'Same escape route tonight?'

'Which route would that be?' Alfred looked at him with interest, a fragment of cabbage still snagged in his goatee.

'You really don't remember, do you? This one's worse than usual.' As they reached the end of the corridor, Alfred took him by the arm and led him quickly through a curtain and into an unlit room. At the end of that room was a door with only an ancient lift-up metal handle to close it. Alfred opened the door. It was dark outside.

'And remember,' Alfred said as Owen stepped out, 'bring me some news from the other kingdom.'

*

'In amnesia, implicit memory is often left untouched. But I should say something here. We've come to understand that much of what used to be termed amnesia can be a lot more complicated than a single psychological slippage. Sometimes there's a neurophysiological event we call a screen occlusion. It's as though the mind decides to dispense with the whole enmeshed memory system as too much of a burden. It's like steam being released from a boiler. It voids the system of all the pressure that's built up. No mental faculties have been lost, only put into temporary suspension.'

'How temporary?' Sylvie asked, though she didn't really need to.

'No way of knowing. It varies from case to case. Often depends on the extent of the trauma. In most cases the period is relatively short, until at least some form of restoration of memory begins. Often, as I said, the implicit memory can remain pretty much unaffected. So that, for example, a musician would still remember his music, still play his instrument, but he wouldn't be able to find his way to the concert hall, or even remember the last meeting with his wife an hour ago. But he wouldn't get a note wrong in the *Hammerklavier Sonata*, if he'd been able to play it before the onset of the amnesia.

'It's a paradox, a riddle, this relationship between explicit and implicit memory. Implicit memory seems to be in some cases largely imperturbable. Certain motor functions, certain skills. Some things, certain structures of the mind, are not displaced by amnesia, even anterograde amnesia.

'Claparède's drawing-pin experiment established that. The patient knew that a concealed sharp point was going to hurt her. She remembered the pain the following day, even though she couldn't remember the visit.'

'So what's Owen's sharp point then?'

'Either what's closing him down or what will open him up again. Often they're both the same thing.'

'Pretty certain I know what it is, either way.' She looked at the young doctor in his white coat; steel-rimmed glasses, a professional smile. She wondered what his wife was like. What a clean life they must lead. Maybe not.

'Where is he?'

'St Clare's. The hostel where he always goes. Amnesia Hotel, I call it. I phoned up. Even arranged for them to put some money in his pocket so he doesn't have to steal. No point bringing him here again, I suppose?'

The doctor shook his head. 'The pattern seems so established by now, doesn't it? After a few weeks his memory will return in full like last time.' He was turning over his notes. 'Three years ago. Five years ago. Seven years ago. Unless the trauma was something notably worse. Wouldn't want to give him any drugs, in any case: he seems to have developed his own techniques for displacing the centre of his nervous system, as it is.'

As she was leaving he put his hand on her shoulder. Such a gentle touch, not like Owen's gripping urgency. Medical not marital.

'One thing I never got to the bottom of with him. Owen's mother. What was she, exactly?'

'A succubus.' She had turned to face him. She was smiling now; he wasn't. A tiny curl of brown hair beneath his right nostril registered a failure in shaving that morning. The tiniest wisp.

'Is she still with us?'

'Not physically, no.'

*

Owen walked along the canal and then up on the city walls. Now the water was beneath him, catching lights the city threw away. He looked up at the sky. There were gods up there, amongst the wreckage of their ancient implements. Ploughs, nets, tridents. He walked on beneath the glowing graveyard. Stepped into a pub. A mesh of smoke, words like trapped animals tangled inside it. Laughter sharpened into blades. Finally he was back at the hostel.

Alfred sat on the other bed counting out pills from a bottle into the palm of his hand. And Owen started to speak, without considering the words at all.

'Quite a number of people think that medicine must be nauseous and drastic if it is to do them any good. They take strong, violent, stomach-irritating purgatives when a small dose of Holloway's Pills would restore them to perfect health without the least inconvenience or distress. Holloway's Pills suit the most delicate stomach. They are easy and agreeable to take and they never cause any griping pain, but quickly and effectively eject all impurities from the system. That is why they will suit you if you suffer from indigestion, constipation, biliousness, flatulence, or any stomach, liver or kidney disorder. Try them today and get both immediate relief and a permanent cure. But where there is rheumatism, gout or any kindred complaint, Holloway's Ointment should be used in conjunction with the pills.'

'Where did that come from?' Alfred asked.

'I don't know.' Owen was sitting on the other bed, startled at his own little speech.

'Word for word, I should think. A sign in a pharmacist's window. I remember them.'

'What?'

'Holloway's Pills. When I was a boy. You don't though. Too young. Done a lot of reading, I think, Owen, in your time.

Probably too much. Should stick to this.' Alfred held up the leather-bound Bible. 'But then I seem to remember you've read that too, haven't you? Or bits of it anyway. Research, was it, different tattoos for different hides? You'd better get some sleep.'

The next day after breakfast Owen went out alone again. This time he let the ticket in his pocket guide him to Chester Library. He found a Bible, Alfred's book, and hunted through it quickly in a flurry. God, he thought, seems to be a much-unrequited lover, so angry at the faithlessness of his little darlings. And with every lethal shakedown another book gets added to his scripture. More deaths; more forgiveness. He keeps setting things up so they can love Him, obey His commandments, live in peace. And they keep killing one another. Always killing one another. Owen moved on. He felt a strange craving to open other books.

Shakespeare: he looked into that large volume for more than an hour. It seemed that reality was elusive until it donned a mask; identity gained its energy by translating itself. So where had he been translated from, then? Could it really be true that a man must put an antic disposition on, so as to madden himself into action? Owen had been here before, hadn't he, just as he had been on the city walls before. Just as he'd walked beneath the shining emblems in the sky before. He went over to the other shelf.

Picked up a book called *Autobiography* by Charles Darwin. A sad man lost the most beloved member of his family, his daughter. He could no longer hear her beguiling speech. So he searched and searched through all the family archives until he arrived at ancestors with no speech at all. Then ones behind them with no souls. Beyond those were others who had no tongues. Then ones with no heads. Headless molluscs. What a melancholy genealogy. What kind of science could yearn for such amnesiac parents? Amnesiac. Now why was that word such a prompt to memory? Suddenly Owen had to be out in the air.

He stared across the square at a window filled with ghost-brides, wrapped in white cotton, satin and silk. The Havisham Room: it filled him with dread, a dread he had no words for. What had he not done to those manikins? He walked across to the cathedral gate and before he even arrived he could hear it. The laughter, the cheering, the shouting, even though no one there was actually laughing or cheering or shouting, only leaving their traces back and forth in a mangle of space. Here was Alfred's other kingdom. Here's where the mysteries had all been played out.

A white plastic bag flipped and dawdled before catching the wind and trundling along once more: a transient ghost in its ill-fitting shroud.

'And you could see them?' Alfred asked later.

'I could see them.'

'God and Lucifer.'

'Both.'

'Ranulph Higden.'

'Who?'

'Ranulph Higden, Monk of Chester. And the author of *Poly-chronicon*. He wrote them, so they say anyway. Even went to see the Pope to get permission for the performances. The Chester Mystery Plays. You could have seen the things you saw five hundred years ago every Whitsuntide. On the other hand, you could have seen them last year. You couldn't have seen them today, though. Most people forget the past, Owen, but you manage to forget the present. Your amnesia forms a little hole that lets the past come back to fill it, from however far away. But the present won't let you alone for long, you know. She always seems to come back to get you.'

The next day he left early, wandering in and out of the shops, a vagrant, a revenant of his own curiosity. Instruments, confections, garments: they were all slotting back in place now. The cupboard of invisible objects inside him was filling up again. The present's inventory. He stood before the antique jeweller's window: so many lives in those little gleaming emblems. Engagement rings, wedding rings pawned off after death or divorce. The ouroboros of love. What was that? He couldn't remember. A snake with its tail in its mouth? Was that what he was? Eating the endless circle of himself? There was even an eternity ring. He only hoped death had brought that one here. Otherwise eternity was so short it didn't even last for one lifetime. He went into the music shop. Watching, listening, observing once more the reality he seemed to have recently exited.

The shop assistant was silently observing an older man as he picked up one of the nastiest items in the whole shop: miniature bongos, a ten-pound piece of nonsense, constructed out of cheap plastics somewhere in the ill-paid depths of industrial China. The old man in the raincoat tapped at them tentatively, as though a couple of tiny mammals might still be locked inside. Dwarf marmosets, perhaps, thought Owen. Or Gobi rats.

'What's the skin on these?' the man enquired gravely.

'Mongolian warthog,' the assistant replied without missing a beat. 'Yak supplies have been pitiful this year.'

'How do they compare?'

'The warthog with the yak?'

'Yes.'

'Aficionados claim the skin softens quicker. You might need to re-tighten them every eighteen months. Easier on the old fingers though. For the more intimate numbers. Tito Puente wouldn't have anything else next to his palms, so I've heard.'

'And he was good, was he?'

'The best.'

'I'll take them.'

'Big gig, is it?' the assistant asked as he rang up the till.

'Sorry?'

'I was wondering if Sir needed the miniature plastic Chinese bongos for a forthcoming musical event. Or is it merely a matter of private pleasure?'

'Oh, they're not for me. My grandson.'

'And how old is the little man?'

'Five. But I always try to get him something decent.'

'Yes, it's so important, isn't it? Imagine how different life would have been if the youthful Miles Davis, asking the old man for something to blow, had been given a comb and a piece of toilet paper, instead of that beautiful trumpet.' The assistant was looking straight at Owen, who was recovering another skill from time's abyss: he had finally remembered how to smile.

'Did he say Alpha and Omega?' Alfred asked him later at the hostel.

'The one called God did, yes.'

'He called himself Alpha and Omega?'

'And the other one called himself Lucifer. He talked about the light.'

'That's what his name means, Owen: Lucifer, bearer of light. I think you might have known that once. Angels are bright still, though the brightest fell.'

He was on the city walls again. He was part of a story, like every stone beneath his feet, but he didn't know the plot. He stared down. The bridge of sighs. Beneath that the dead men's room, hewn from rock, stinking, fetid, domicile of rats and prisoners awaiting execution, ultimate confinement before ultimate indignity. And Little Ease, a cell the size of a man, reducible even further by boards employed upon the uncooperative miscreant. Less than the size of a man now, but still with a man inside it. Pit and pendulum. An iron glove at hand for the coaxing. The drop. The hanging. The twitching exhibition. The crowd eating, jeering, perhaps even mourning sometimes. How did he know all this?

A little further on he stopped and stared at the old stone warehouse. He remembered the lights swinging inside it. That's where the other mystery play had been performed, wasn't it? He could hear the woman screaming. He knew what they were doing to her; he had set them on to do it, after all. He was responsible for this. He could almost see her face. Almost. He could feel her body. And he had caused it: he had brought the catastrophe about. This much he knew for certain – her pain was his creation. He felt cold all the way through to his bones, sick with himself. He walked quickly to the hostel and there, seeing him shivering on the bed, Alfred reached under his own bed and took out the whiskey bottle, which was forbidden. He smiled as he handed it to Owen, the leather Bible still clutched in his other hand.

Translucent gold, it was, hydrogen to helium in a big burn, a blaze in your throat that soon became a blaze in your mind and heart. They called her Deva, the fort and the river whose coils still held the town so tightly. The goddess. The holy one. Often hungry. She swallowed men whole in her battles. Young women big with child swayed back and forth among her weeds, the mother dead while the child still clamoured for life inside her. Why was that part of the mystery play? He felt the pull of the cold snake of the ancient river, but he could feel the hot god too. He poured another whiskey into the tumbler.

'Do you know what it was this time?' Alfred asked, finally.

'No.'

He reached down once more under the bed and pulled out a newspaper. 'Take another drink, Owen. Take a big one this time.' Owen did as he was told, then Alfred placed the newspaper on his lap and Owen stared down at the picture of the young woman and the caption beneath it. He put down the whiskey, stood up and left the room. At the bottom of the corridor he went into the bathroom and stared at the mirror.

His face was the map of a country too many people had overrun. The rivers of gold were polluted already with prospectors' boots. Frightened beasts were heading for the highlands, followed by bullets.

City of Ghosts

Sylvie Treadle was Sylvie Ashton again. That wasn't to say she had divorced Owen; she hadn't. But despite the legal entity *Mrs S. Treadle*, who still received sundry communications from one authority or another, she now thought of herself entirely as Ms Ashton. She marvelled at what had once been her readiness, for a time anyway, to relinquish that identity. She was once more Sylvie Ashton and would remain so unto death, even though she shared a house in Chester with Owen Treadle. When he was there.

And now she was on her way to Liverpool, to the Signum Institute where she worked. She had already telephoned to check that Owen was still safely berthed in the hostel. She had arranged to leave a little more money for him. She accelerated away as the traffic cleared. He always wore that old RAF greatcoat he'd picked up in a sale somewhere. She had tried to dump it more than once, but he insisted on keeping it, down in the cellar along with the dead books and the defunct film cans. And whenever he went missing on one of his walkabouts, that coat went missing with him. The amnesiac's greatcoat, a cover for the great wound of remembrance. A vast serge made for a modern Icarus but ending up on earth-bound Owen instead. Bloody Owen. At least he wasn't belly-up in the river, in the old bitch's maw. That was always the first thing she checked. She sometimes wondered if it might have been simpler if he had been. Down amongst the weeds, where everything's forgotten.

The Signum on Rodney Street was only a few doors along from the Institute of Western Acupuncture. Signum was not quite as dilapidated as that Georgian building, slowly mouldering back towards humanity's original organic dwelling-place, but it was far from spruce. In fact it was stained, despite the copious rain. The Cathedral, Paddy's Wigwam, had once more stuck the spikes of its famous, modernist rotunda into the sky and the heavens had been duly punctured. Pious pre-cipitation, Father. Rain covered the city. The docks were wet, the roofs were wet, the streets were wet and the people were wet. Not that they looked too hang-dog about it: they'd got used to being rained-on. Liverpool is a city of cargoes, and so, like the hold of any cargo ship, it is often half-submerged.

She remembered how John Lennon had sat on the Albert Dock in the early morning inside that soft insistent rain and heard the *basso profundo* of a ship in the Mersey mist. He'd heard the call of the Atlantic, the USA, the glitter of the future. And what could she hear? The plaintive drone of Lennon's voice, a noise that was surely death's insistence against the come-hitherish vocal curlicues of Paul McCartney. A descant on the inescapability of night.

John was singing now, on her car's tape player: *Don't Let Me Down*. It was pretty evident it wasn't Yoko he was singing to, but life itself, and the urgency of his tone was maintained so compellingly because he knew life would indeed let him down, since it always does. Time is on death's side, that's why the hooded figure always looks so relaxed about each forthcoming contest. John knew this in his heart of hearts, and the know-ledge still came through in his singing, despite all that arty prattle with Yoko, the hair-growing for peace, the lengthy week-end bed-malingerings of sincerity. He knew it and the know-ledge simply wouldn't go away. The bullet was already flying. That was why the music stayed with us now; the tunes, the image, the voice, so long after the man had gone. One more image from the city of ghosts, then. This was the nature of her research. This was her work at the Signum Institute. The afterlife of images: how they mapped the mind's ravaged landscape, like trenches and barbed wire on the Western Front. How we couldn't live without them any more. Why was Liverpool so laden with ghosts and their images? And why did they sometimes seem more real than the living?

The afterlife of images: that was her work. The title of her thesis, the title of several essays in *The Burlington Magazine*, *The Journal of the Warburg and Courtauld Institutes*, *Modern Painters*. It was the title of the main course she taught at the Signum Institute, and many of the lectures she gave at home and abroad. It would be the title of her book too when it was finally finished. And it might as well have been the name of her room, because that creaky attic on the top floor, though capable of holding seminars of up to eight at a time, really only embraced the images inside it and they were the images that went to make up their own afterlife. Labyrinths, paintings, photographs, cinematic stills, holograms, and a huge Wurlitzer rainbow, a gaudy spectrum of the gaps between the quantum states. All around the walls of her room, jammed into every spare inch of each bookshelf, even in the corners on the floor, were images, and all the images were so dense with information that she could often sit in here in silence for hours at a time and look around her. That's if she was permitted to do so, which she seldom was. She glanced at the timetable she'd pasted on her door. Nothing until the afternoon. That was a relief. A few hours of serious thought. The anxiety about Owen had finally abated. Well almost. It was the same as before. Something bad happened. Owen's mind decided the events were too dark to be coped with in the conscious state, so it sent all the information elsewhere. Then Owen sent himself elsewhere, anywhere his wife wasn't. Or whatever makeshift wife he'd recently been toying with. There was a knock on the door. Alison peered around it. Tiny moon face, glasses hanging off her nose, shoulders, as ever, hunched.

'Any news on Owen?'

'He's all right. At the hostel. Give him a week, maybe less. He'll be home, don't worry. The usual routine.'

'Can I do anything?'

'Not really, Ali. Thanks. I wouldn't mind seeing that video Charlie made of the crippled girl some time.' A hand fluttered its condolent fingers round the door and her tiny friend was gone.

She had met Owen while he was in Liverpool making the film *City of Ghosts*. It was a decade after the shooting down of Lennon in the streets of New York. Owen was technically the writer, Sue Granville the director, since he hadn't yet teamed up with Johnny Tamworth, but it was soon evident that it was Owen's project. Sylvie looked out of the window down towards the Albert Dock and remembered the first time she had seen the film, at a screening at the university. She had asked him afterwards how he had achieved the curious dream-like quality of the black-and-white sequences.

'I got Sue to shoot it all at dawn, and slightly underexpose the footage. We filmed from the back of a truck, told the driver to hold a constant speed. So it's like those Atget pictures of Paris: mostly deserted, the scene of a crime after the criminal's escaped. Call it the landscape of Lennon's mind after our quarryman had escaped this city for the last time. Imagine the imagination of a dead man. Part prison; part cemetary; part dreamscape. Maybe it's the same with the imagination of a living man. Remember the weirdness of *Strawberry Fields Forever*. So we were looking at Liverpool through Lennon's eyes after the man was already dead.'

When the soundtrack wasn't filled with Lennon's music it

was filled with Owen's script, an odd, surreal montage of impressions, biographies, elegies, notes for love songs to women and places. This was someone who seemed to understand the relationship between image and word, which was precisely what she'd been working on at the time; the truth was, it was what she'd always been working on. She was still working on it now too: the afterlife of images is always situated in language. It was pretty obvious Owen was sleeping with Sue, simply from the way she touched him from time to time, but he didn't give any indication that this was likely to prevent him from sleeping with anyone else. And it didn't. Three months later he moved into her house in Chester, the house she had bought from the money she inherited after her father's death. She had been about to sell it, since she had realised that she couldn't really afford to maintain it by herself.

'Don't sell it,' Owen had said, after he'd spent an hour with her there. 'I'll help you keep it.' And he had. His work on scripts, treatments, and the television films he now made with John Tamworth, had always kept coming in. The Tamworth-Treadle collaborations had been highly acclaimed. Commissions had followed. Their television features were sometimes given independent screenings in art cinemas, more in Europe than in Britain, but they made it on to the small screen all over the world. He couldn't be criticised on the financial front. He'd paid his way. Even a little stretch of her way too, from time to time. She looked at the photograph of him above her desk. Black hair, a face simultaneously delicate and strong. The darkest, largest eyes she'd ever seen, apart from the photographs of a certain Spanish painter. Black holes through which the world disappeared. In more ways than one sometimes. The afterlife of images.

She decided to stay the night at the Signum. She had a little sofabed over by the window, which she occasionally used. She surely deserved one night left entirely to herself, without the luminous silence of the telephone crouching six inches from her ear.

Hamish was around at seven asking when she was planning on leaving.

'I'm staying the night.'

'You should really inform security beforehand.'

'I thought you were security these days.'

'Well, in a manner of speaking.'

'I shan't be in too late and I shan't be bringing any boys back, I promise. It'll just be me and you here. We can listen to each other typing.'

Hamish Flyte was something of a mystery himself. As far as anyone could recall he had originally arrived at the Institute on an accounting assignment, but had subsequently made himself so invaluable to the Signum, becoming a member of every significant committee and a controlling figure over every aspect of the Institute's slightly unfathomable finances, that no one could now see a way of getting rid of him, though many would have liked to. He was not popular, and was only too aware of the fact. That was why he had installed a scan-and-trap software programme which could gain access to all incoming or outgoing internet texts or email communications. In the event of certain phrases occurring, the screened passage would become available to Hamish through his exclusive monitoring system.

He had claimed to the other directors that this was an unfortunate necessity, a result of a residual racial clot in Liverpool's cultural arteries, a disfigurement still capable of affecting even so healthy a body as the Signum Institute, because, Hamish claimed, of the mental conflicts which three centuries of slavery, immigration, emigration and religious strife had between them generated on Merseyside. In fact he was primarily if not solely concerned with any references made to the diminutive stature, combative personality and geographical origins of the present Director of Studies. Himself, in fact. So the Racial Epithet Catchment Enumerator (RECE for short) would surely have appeared unexpectedly specific to anyone other than Hamish who might have gained access to it, which no else in fact ever could, since he had ensured that he was in possession of the only monitoring trigger. The lexicon of sought-for phrases which he trawled daily, and usually nightly too, included 'malignant Hiberian dwarf', 'Glaswegian toad', 'kilted wanker', 'Jockstrap Willie', 'Scotch Midget', 'masturbating Pict', 'Clydeside Chlamydia' and 'Gorbals Gonad'. He was entirely convinced that such disobliging phrases were continuously passing back and forth through the ether, but he could never manage to nail a specific user. He knew what they said about him: he didn't need telling. He'd always known. He'd get one of them one day. But for now they were managing inexplicably to evade his scrutiny. He often saw them huddling together at the bottom of corridors, trying to hide their giggles and guffaws as he approached. He wondered if they might have dreamt up some sort of code. An inserted semi-colon perhaps, to facilitate the disparagement of his own still semi-colonised land and those engendered there? Or full-stops inserted, just the simple minuscule black mark in the middle of certain words, perhaps? He tried it out on the scanner: *Toe.rag. Scum.bag. Dick.head. Shit.face.*

Still nothing. Evidently something more exotic and encrypted then: they were a hieroglyphic lot at the Signum Institute. He knew that well enough. *Bast.ards.*

Thus it was that while Sylvie finally switched off the light and stared out over the Mersey and its mighty ships, Hamish click-clicked on his keyboard with quiet determination four doors away. She switched the light back on for a moment to look at one of the pictures pinned to her wall. In the art of Laos, the river-dragon itself is indistinguishable from the river. Those spumes, fumes, flushes; those fanged rushes; those meanders . . . And yet there was something she was trying to focus. The river god was sluggish, dark, possessive where the nymph was quick, light, constantly escaping. Where did that leave Deva then? Had she combined them both in one? She switched the light off again. The waters of Lethe at last: they were the ones that brought forgetfulness.

When she arrived back the following evening in Cathedral Close, Chester, the lights in the house were on. As she opened the door she heard the soundtrack of the film. She knew it only too well. Owen was back and was watching *City of Ghosts*. It seemed an appropriate choice for his return trip into his own dark time. He was re-acquainting himself with his work, finding out what might be contained in his head. She walked into the room quietly. Lennon's lugubrious tones were lamenting his inability to go back to the place of his birth because of all the drug-charges against him. Owen looked up from the armchair and smiled. Anyone would think he'd popped out to the shop fifteen minutes before, to buy some red peppers.

'Back then, Owen.'

'I always come back.' A cargo ship bleated through the mist and Lennon's voice came over the soundtrack once more, disparaging one old comrade, annihilating another.

'Reminding yourself who you are?'

'I thought I was reminding myself who someone else was. But let's not quibble.'

She made him shower and shave, then let him come to bed.

He stared down at himself rising. His body had memories that his mind had lost. It was veined with memories.

'This has happened before, you know.'

'I don't know.'

'I do know, Owen. And it has.'

'Even this.'

'Even this. It's you on day release from repetition. Your little wormhole out of consciousness.'

A little wormhole. Eve's little wormhole. That was in the mystery play, wasn't it? He felt her flesh and clutched it tightly. Closing his eyes at last, praying tonight there would be no dreams.

In the morning she left him sleeping. She went down to the cellar and saw the greatcoat hanging from its rusty hook. Out of the pocket you could just make out the newspaper Alfred had given him. She lifted it out and saw the image of the young woman's face. That was enough. She didn't need to read any of the words.

Living on Air

Keep pushing on towards the headland. What had begun as inanition was now transmuting to energy inside her. It was true, everything Lady Pneuma had told her was true: food was an impurity, a bodily impurity for an impure spirit. With the spiritual cleansing came physical redemption too. She might need tiny fragments for now, morsels to assuage the wren of contamination still fluttering inside her. But even that would soon be over. Air and water would then suffice. The air, as Pneuma had predicted, now tasted like invisible gold. Never before had she known the taste of gold. All she had to do was find the hut and she could rest. She had made the right decision, she had no doubt about that. Back there, she had become what she had pretended to be. He had written the part for her, and she had given her soul to it, even though he had lied. The contaminated always lie. They live on lies; that's what they eat. The Delta Programme had established that all she now needed was to commit herself entirely to breathing divinity and thereby being sustained within it. In the little bothie, she shredded the wrappers from the Bounty bar to make a tiny fire. So insubstantial, its ashes. So little was needed for a flame either inside or out. Those wrappers were the last contact she would have with material food. The last clearing finally beckoned.

Once we lived on light and the *anima* inside us fed on nothing at all but air, and took its sufficiency from such elemental provender. Only the corruption of the spirit had led to the material distraction of food. Alex had decided to make her way back to that primordial state where we swallowed air as the glow-worm does, and the soul generates its own electricity, a little bulb gleaming inside the lampshade of the body. Lady Pneuma had done it now for ten years, and Alex had never seen a healthier looking human being. She needed nothing but air, not even water any more.

Soon her own exhausted body was lying on the makeshift bed. It was growing dark. The air was chilling. She focused entirely on air. Owen Treadle was an impurity, like food, the mind's soiled food, left entirely behind her. She was shedding the skin of her disastrous former life, and what she had been made to do inside it. She was being re-born, free now of the entanglement of dark matter.

*

As the disciple lay so far to the north eating air, the object of her devotion sat in her rooms in the Claymore Hotel staring out of the window, down at the traffic moving slowly along Piccadilly. Lady Pneuma, *aka* Rachel Askarli, had begun her spiritual journey twenty years before in Bermondsey, when she had noticed a coin outside a confectioner's shop. She had not picked up the coin, but had instead stood and watched for ten minutes as people walked over it. Many of them noticed it lying there, but not a single one bent down to pick it up, until she herself did. It was on the table now before her, encased in perspex, a monstrance holding its own demotic host. This coin of small denomination she had shown to her disciples many times: the currency of our civilisation, debased to the point where it could be discarded on the street and left there. Retrieved finally as a spiritual emblem, a memento of the dynamics of triviality.

Her studies had been long and arduous. She had needed to visit the sites of many traditions until the truth had broken through at last, ten years earlier on the first day of May in New York. She had been on the top floor of the Waldorf Hotel in Manhattan, listening to the unearthly siren of the elevator, when all had been made clear. She could never have formulated it herself. It was a gift.

We had let ourselves fall into the realm of dark matter. We had engrossed our spirits with materiality. We had corroded our souls with the food of animals and forgotten that our true realm was in fact the air, Ariel's dimension. We had come to imagine that what we once experienced as no more than a beastly degradation – the consumption of earthly food – was now a necessity. This was the real fall, the one true vertical descent from grace. Its itchy concomitant was all too evident: that the generation of new life required coition, another insalubrious address marked out in the neighbourhood of dark matter. The revelation came on Lady's Day, for that was how the patriarchs of meat had disguised the miracle of the goddess as their own feast, now another festival of the great male schedules of entry and subordination.

From that day on she dressed in blue, Mary's colour, and started to proclaim her philosophy, her revelation, her religion: air nutrition and parthenogenesis. We could live on the nutrients in the air itself and, once the spirit was sufficiently purified, generate life from within ourselves, through the self-intermingling of the spirit. She had written her testament, *The One True Elemental*. Or to speak more truthfully, she had transcribed it. It was published by The Delta Foundation, her movement, the world-wide movement that proclaimed her faith.

And this was the only book which Alex had taken with her to the bothie. She was staring at its pages now as a bad wind headed over from the hills towards her. The Claymore was warm; the bothie very cold. Alex was pale with inanition; Lady Pneuma was bronzed and almost plump from feasting on her unearthly nutrients.

Through the Lens

Owen woke with a blister forming on the skin of his mind. He saw the note propped up against the mirror. *Try to remember who you are, love.*

He washed; he dressed; he went to St. Clare's and walked swiftly down the corridor to Alfred's room. His companion was sitting on the bed with the Bible open on his lap.

'You put a lie inside my mind.'

'No, Owen, I put a truth back inside your mind. You would like to replace that truth with a lie, I think. The replacement would be what most people call forgetting. You're a specialist at that. You've done it before, you know. Usually it was just women. Women you weren't married to. They came and went. This time there's something that can't be forgotten. A woman again. But something different.'

'Why should I believe you?'

'Because I gave you the proof. You put it in your greatcoat pocket. Why aren't you wearing your greatcoat today?' Owen hesitated.

'It's in the cellar.'

'That's where the truth is then, Owen. Back down in the cellar. You've put the truth in the cellar again. Better make sure you don't go down there for a while, until you've fitted the plastic cover back on your memory. The one that keeps the dust out.'

Owen left without another word. He walked along the city

walls. He knew these walls, didn't he? He'd walked them many times, once as a writer, once as someone re-arranging reality, and once as a lover. One of those for whom the world is made new. He couldn't be sure. He went down the steps and found a bar. He didn't want any alcohol. He could still taste the bitterness of Alfred's whisky from two days before, and it was a bad taste. A bad taste that left its traces in the mind. He asked for a mineral water and sat down at the table. Had he already been here? He felt as though he'd been everywhere before. He stared at the woman at the next table. Blonde, mid-thirties, maybe older, looking at her watch and grimacing. She was evidently waiting. He wondered if she knew she kept sighing. Then he arrived finally, the awaited one, all waving arms and sandy hair in his eyes. Younger than her, a lot younger. Not her son though; he could tell that immediately.

'Finally turned up, have you? Good of you to come.'

'If you must know . . . ' God, he could see how much she hated the heart-rending tone this young man could always summon from the wells within, though it must have enchanted her once. ' . . . I was helping a blind person get to the station.' She sighed even more heavily than before.

'You weren't helping a blind person get to the station really, were you Alasdair?' He stared at her, the practised look of hurt in his eyes, rehearsing once more the rubric of his own sincerity. 'I think you were helping a fully-sighted person get pissed. And the fully-sighted person you were helping to get pissed was you. That's what I think. I can smell the beer without even needing to kiss you. In fact, I don't want to kiss you anyway, now I come to think about it.'

His expression glazed, frigid with incomprehension at her lack of charity. How could she so misconstrue him? He reached a hand out gently and touched her arm, as one who might say, 'I have been mistook, but I forgive you, beloved.' She stared at the hand as though it were a massive white slug which had inexplicably materialised upon her sleeve. A vast milky slug with five legs, all covered in tiny hairs.

'At least put your expertise to some use then.' His lips curled down at the edges, trying to shape themselves into a question mark, as she stood up. 'Go buy some wine before they all turn up for lunch, and I'll meet you back at the house. Then we can all get pissed, can't we? And who knows, if you manage to pour enough of it down my throat as well as your own, your luck might change later on. Between the sheets. After you've finished doing the washing-up.'

He stood at the table and hesitated. 'The only thing is . . . ' – eyes screwed up, little boy caught short on his way to school – ' . . . I don't have any money left, babe. Spent it all at the Albion.'

'Then you'd best get to the station quickly and mug that blind man before his train comes in, my darling. Or alternatively, find yourself another bed in which to try your luck tonight. Because I'm not giving you any more this week. I'd rather leave the whole effing lot to the RNIB.'

They went out, untouching. Were all human beings like this? He really couldn't remember. What they had just done with one another struck him as somehow . . . realistic: a vivid representation of themselves. Back on the wall, he walked. He knew these buildings, he knew the houses. Finally he stopped again in sight of the disused warehouse. He knew that building very well, didn't he? All too well. He started to hear the cries in there, the cries of a young woman having her body taken from her, having her body turned inside out, and he turned away quickly, heading for home, unable to listen. They had put a title on that part of *Deva*: The Passion. Outside the house, he halted. A beautiful green car, a Morgan was parked in the street. He ran his hand along the bonnet. That metal so familiar. It was his, wasn't it? He was suddenly sure of it. He let himself into the house and opened the drawer in the hallway table. Keys. He knew those keys all right. He picked them up and walked back out to the car.

He didn't need to think about it. He soon had the engine turning over, then he realised it was sunny. He hadn't thought about it while he was walking, but it was a fine day, so he took the roof down on his convertible car. He would go driving. Where? It didn't matter. The car would find its own way. And it did. With each fresh mile the car reminded him how well they knew one another. It had its own memories, and was generously sharing them. He felt safe in the car; he knew there'd never been any screaming in here. No passion; no mystery play. The wind started to interview him blusteringly, and he answered its questions. He shouted his answers back above the windscreen: 'Speed is how we catch up with the world. If the speed of light is the only ultimate constant in the universe then the closer we can get to it, the closer we are to reality, surely. Why on earth stay still?' He had said all these words before, hadn't he, and to camera? He started laughing. He was in re-play mode. One hour later he arrived in Llandudno. Twenty minutes after that, Llandudno started replaying itself to him.

The straightened-out crescent of the promenade displayed the grand hotels, their bright pastel colours, their genteel imperial names and balconies like the busts of Victorian ladies in full sail. A great line of them stood proud on the shore and stared out to sea. Flags fluttered before the apron of the beach, white flecks of gulls scattered like flashes of limestone outcrop showing through the brown heather and gorse of the Orme. Piebald donkeys dutifully bore that week's children on their backs, and the pier stood above the waves on its cross-barred metal stilts. The cast-iron pavilion of the Grand Hotel had grown rotten and rusty in its ruin and now had the look of seaside archaeology about it. Ancient communal songs drifted over on the salty breeze, seemingly conjured from nowhere. On the pier, giant inflated Disney heads stared down in garish hilarity. A kiosk offered *Adult Novelties and Curiosities* and men in brightly coloured weather suits (no trust in the sun's longevity here) reeled in their lines one by one. Never was a single fish attached. The fishermen changed their sodden lugworms for drier ones, cast out again and stared down once more at the legs of the jetty, grown fanciful over the years with a ragged accrual of mussel-shells. He was staring at the town and watching a film at the same time.

The lens carried on panning. Now the images were black-and-white. Snug in their nest of cedars and beeches in the hills above town, flamboyantly gabled houses kept a wary eye on the latest cargo of grockles, disgorged by the coachload at their designated spots. A British resort hunting for its next patch of sunshine between lashings of rain. Pilgrims so often made for the beach and crouched in meditation inside their waterproof cowls as they stared out at the great grey god of the sea. Distant ships rode its wrinkled back like parasites on the skin of a rhino.

The lens closed its eye momentarily and it was dawn. In a small hotel by the slanted tramway a woman woke suddenly. She leapt from the bed in answer to the rapping at the door. Only as she stood in her flimsy shift with the sound still in her ears did she realise that it was the harsh regularity of soldiers marching. She went back to the bed and lay still on her back. Such a short honeymoon. Small resort. Small hotel. Small man, but a good one. God, let him come back alive. Finally she sank into sleep, as the herring-gulls start shrieking a few feet from her half-opened window. How he had loved that body, that face, the little oval of moonflesh. Her husband had gone, already gone, one of the brave boys leaving with the

British Expeditionary Forces. The tangled sheets still seemed pungent with his absence. This was all film now. Owen knew this, because all these images moving through his head were black-and-white. He had invented this. He had invented the woman, though he had needed a real one to do it. And he knew where to find the hotel too. Ten minutes later he stood in the reception area.

'Want the same room as usual, Mr Treadle?'

'I'll have the same room, yes.'

'By yourself this time, are you? I'll just check you in and then get you the key.' Same lenses in her spectacles as the woman in the café; same underwater look to the jellyfish eyes. I'm ringing another bell, he thought. Wherever I go I ring bells. Owen the campanologist.

Once inside the room, lying on the bed, clutching at memories he knew were still there, despite the fresh linen, he recognised the woman in the film. First they had made love here, hadn't they, he and the woman – not on film, that part – then they had filmed her there, lamenting the passing of a mythical man. A mythical man representing so many real ones. And where was she now? Where was Alex now? He knew that fact and yet he didn't know it; he both knew it and blanked it out at the same time. A self-cancelling memory then. Something it might be better to keep in the cellar with your greatcoat. He slept. How long for? When he woke he searched his pockets for the mobile, but it wasn't there. He did have one somewhere, didn't he, but he didn't know where. He needed to talk to Sylvie. He left the hotel and walked down the street until he found a telephone booth. She picked up the phone after five tones.

'Where are you, Owen?'

'Llandudno.'

'Revisiting all your memories in a hurry, it seems.'

'I made a film here.' There was a pause. This time he put the question-mark in. 'Didn't I make a film here?'

'Yes, Owen, you made *Time's Widow* there, remember. You don't actually make the films, love; you write them, though Johnny says your scripting is so specific that it's often you who has decided exactly where the camera will be pointing at any particular moment. He used to mind but he doesn't seem to bother much any more, since the pair of you have won so many prizes. So many shining prizes. He phoned half an hour ago, by the way, to see how you were.'

'Johnny.'

'John Tamworth. The director you collaborated with. On all your classic television features.'

'Was there one about speed? Did I talk in it once, driving a car?'

'*Catching Up With The Earth*. It's here on the shelf, next to *City of Dreams*'

'What was the last one I did?'

'*Deva*.'

'*Deva*.'

'But that one hasn't been released. That's the one that seems to have cost you your memory again. It's not out yet, but Johnny will be turning up with a DVD any day now. I think that must have been the one that made a widow of time's lonely widow. So young to be a widow, too. Poor little mite. Poor little Alex. Are you coming back, Owen?'

'Not tonight, no. I need to find something out.'

'You need to find a lot of things out, Owen, I don't doubt that, but I'm not sure you'll do any of it in a hotel in Llandudno. Not during one night. Are you alone, out of interest?'

'Not sure.'

'Have a look behind you then. Close your eyes and hold out

your hands. See if there's any flesh within groping distance that doesn't feel like yours.'

'There's no one here, physically. That doesn't mean I'm alone though, does it, Sylvie?'

'Sounds like a line from one of your scripts. I daresay it will be before long.' Ten seconds of silence. 'You're not coming back tonight then?'

'Not tonight, no.'

'Have a nice time.' And she hung up.

The Riverside Gallery

Sylvie stared for a moment at the phone. She walked into the kitchen and poured herself a glass of dry white wine from the fridge. Chardonnay, its flavour always a little too insistent without food to counter it, but she didn't feel like eating. After one sip, she went over to the cellar door, opened it and walked down the steps. Something cold and unwelcoming about that cellar; she'd rather not go down there at all. Always a damp feeling to the stone. The light had gone years before, and no one had ever bothered to fix it. She stopped at the bottom and stared at Owen's greatcoat. The tip of the tabloid newspaper stuck out of the pocket. No, she'd had enough of this. None of it was her doing, was it, so how come Owen had abandoned the memory and left it to her, like some dark inheritance she was meant to sort out? Down here in the cellar of their lives. Was she the archivist of his memory, then? Bloody Owen. Came back here to her bed for one night, as though she were some sort of service station, then off down the road on his memory-recovery programme.

She walked quickly back up the stairs, slammed the cellar door, walked into the kitchen, downed the glass of wine in one gulp and then poured herself another. She went over to the phone, picked it up and dialled a number. She didn't need to look it up. After a few rings, the voice came on, cultured, slow and warm. Henry.

'The Riverside Gallery. How may I help you?'

'It's me.'

'So how is he?'

'In fucking Llandudno, recovering his memories, almost certainly the wrong ones, I should think, knowing Owen. I'm mighty sick of most of mine at the moment, I can tell you. Particularly the ones containing the word Owen. Be more than happy to dump the lot.'

'Want to come over?' She hesitated.

'Is it all right?'

'I'll get rid of all the belly dancers and temple prostitutes, change the silk sheets and . . . bingo.'

'You're on.'

'Take-away?'

'As long as we can have it in the Picasso Room.'

'Have to be pizza then. Pablo might rise from his Iberian grave if there were to be a smell of curry in there.'

'Pizza is fine. Pink period for me. You can have the blue. Make mine vegetarian, remember. Don't want to be having bad dreams. Not with so many minotaurs about.'

'What time?'

'I'll have a shower, then set off. About an hour and a half.'

She cleaned herself up, chose some nice clothes, black silk, white cotton. Old-fashioned erotica. Henry was very predictable in some ways, and at this moment she was grateful for the fact.

She stripped slowly in front of the mirror. Item after item of clothing came off, and she tried to see herself as a man might see her. Until the delta itself was revealed and he had no choice now but to enter. The mirror was a man looking. Owen, for example.

And was that how Alex Gregory had done it? No, her attraction was to be taken surely, not to offer herself at all.

To be taken. Owen had seen that, and that was precisely how he had used her, in both *Time's Widow* and *Deva*. She'd had the clothes taken from her both times.

Naked now, Sylvie stared at the mirror, which stared back.

'I hate you, Owen Treadle. And the way you use people to turn them into images. I don't care how good the images are. That's not what human beings are for. It's not what that girl was for. You took the food right out of her mouth.'

Why can't mirrors cry? They do, of course, but only do it if you go first.

She walked back into the bedroom and looked at the photograph of herself and Owen on the dressing table. Nine inches higher than her own head, Owen's black throw of hair and dark eyes were the first thing to strike you. But Sylvie repaid her own close attention, that almost blonde hair combed back from a face of delicate features, green eyes, small sharp nose. Vivacious: that's how her features had been described more than once. The laughing girl, they'd called her; that was before her marriage. Tiny lines had started mapping the years at the edges of her eyes since that shot had been taken. Hardly surprising, really. And she was perhaps a few pounds heavier these days, but still very attractive. If she ever had any doubts about that, the next fellow down the line trying to get her into bed soon removed them. As she pulled her stockings on, she started smiling. Putting things on with such care so someone else can take them off with the same attention later. She found the symmetry pleasing. Sylvie Treadle was going to be entirely Sylvie Ashton tonight.

A little over an hour after climbing into her car she arrived at the riverside road in Shrewsbury where Henry had his gallery.

The Riverside Gallery had become Henry's when his third and most tranquil marriage had ended with his wife's death. Eleanor had been considerably older and not in the best of health from the start. Henry always spoke of her with warmth and affection, but Sylvie couldn't help wondering if he might have married the gallery as much as the woman. Anyway, it was now his to do with as he chose. A large white building with black wooden cladding, it was a curious warren of mis-shaped rooms, and low-hung rafters. Henry had divided it up into sections for the public, where he hung his saleable wares, and those parts where you needed special permission to enter, like the living quarters, the kitchen, the bedroom and, most of all, the Picasso Room. The pictures on the wall in there were very much not for sale. Sylvie parked her little car in the drive, looked at the river for a moment, the river that was the cause of so many of Henry's nightmares, and then pushed open the large door, ringing the bell as she walked through.

Physically, Henry was everything that Owen wasn't. Did that apply mentally too? She wasn't sure about that. Where Owen was tall and thin, Henry was short and, not fat exactly, but loose about the waist. He had the unbuttoned look of a Regency Lord. And Henry's hair had greyed all round its untrimmed edges. He was drinking red wine, as usual. After kissing her smilingly (why did Owen always seem to frown when he kissed?) he offered her a glass, which she took.

'The river is behaving itself.'

'For the moment. I still think we'll probably get a chance to test the new defences before long. Shall we go and sit in the Picasso Room then?'

'If I'm still allowed.'

'You're always allowed, you know that.'

'It's a privilege.'

'It certainly is.'

It had begun when Henry had first moved in to the gallery with Eleanor. She had already managed to buy three of the etchings from the *Vollard Suite*, two of them featuring the minotaur that so obsessed Picasso throughout his life. And the same images soon started to obsess Henry too. When his wife had finally died, and the resources of the gallery had become his in their entirety, he had pursued these images with some determination. Picasso etchings were not as expensive as much of his other work. Henry now had all fifteen of the *Vollard Suite* prints which featured the minotaur, and they filled the walls of the Picasso Room. Minotaurs and the women they consumed, or were in their turn consumed by.

'How do you know they're authentic, out of interest?'

'Well, the first look tells me usually. But if I need to check there's the watermark. Some say Vollard; some Picasso, unless it's one of the fifty copies on Montval paper watermarked *Papeterie Montgolfier a Montval*. They're all distinctive. Then there's the sizes, of course: either $13\,^3/_8$ of an inch by $17\,^5/_{16}$ or $15\,^1/_8$ by $19\,^{11}/_{16}$.'

'You're showing off, Henry.'

'I know. But they haven't tended to sell at huge prices over the years, so it would be unlikely for someone to go to all the trouble of an elaborate forgery for something they wouldn't be making all that much money out of. It's all rudimentary Sherlock Holmes stuff. But the ones in this room are authentic, you can take my word for that.'

It was in fact these images that had introduced Henry to Sylvie in the first place. Owen had made a film with John called *Inside the Cave*. It was characteristically clever and wide-ranging. Images from the caves at Lascaux and Chauvet were interspersed with related images from much later in history, and the most related image of all was Picasso's minotaur, a votive offering to that labyrinth of confusion which constitutes a man's life, mind and body. At least that's what she thought the film meant. Owen and Johnny's films never exactly spelt themselves out, and Owen would never discuss them much. Anyway, it had been the kind of subject that intrigued her, given her own studies of the image and its afterlife. She had been around during the shoot at the Riverside and so had inevitably met the proprietor, one Henry Allardyce; she had even asked if she might come to his gallery some time after the filming had ended, to study these images from the *Vollard Suite* when they had a little more stillness about them. She had explained her work; even hinted, not too subtly, that it was from her work that the idea for the film had come, which was almost certainly true. A tiny acknowledgment at the bottom of the film credits hinted at this, though it had never seemed to her to be a sufficient admission of the debt. And she had arrived here one late afternoon with her notebook and pen, while Owen was off with Johnny filming somewhere in Romania. Henry had sat looking at her with an expression of undisguised longing, which she needed at the time, and it had all begun that night.

If you had come in through the main gallery, this is what you would have seen. A lovely little Peter Lanyon, still probably underpriced; a sort of semi-abstract portrait in oils of a coastline, the boats rendered flat and diagrammatic and yet the whole some-how dynamic and surging. A Nolan Rimbaud; African desert miscegenated with the Australian outback, and a man who was half-animal, half-poet. Some curious early works of David Jones which another dealer had had to unload in a hurry. Early charcoals by Gaudier-Brzeska of a dancer. A Craigie Aitchison crucifixion, with a sunset as geometrized as a pyramid behind it. Christ's arms bore brightly coloured birds which appeared to be singing to him. Never had death by ritual torture looked so enchanting. All sorts of modern half-abstract sculptures. A maze of Ayrton's, which you could look down on like Daedalus. But something happened along the corridor separating this gallery from the Picasso Room. Sylvie sensed the shift each time she came. A corridor leading to a cave.

She looked hard at the blinded minotaur led away by a girl with a face like a blazing candle. So many hairy men, their animality touched momentarily with sublimity by the beauty of the female shape they contemplate. All the dark mysteries of life, the endless death and birth which Picasso took as his subject matter. Man, he seems to say, is a minotaur, a courtier, a bullfighter, an artist. He studies the woman to understand the mystery of entering another human being, to fathom the unfathomable mystery of creation. He becomes Rembrandt, he becomes Ingres, he becomes a bull hunted to death. But the woman doesn't have to become anything except what she is. That was what Picasso seemed to think. Sylvie would have begged to differ.

There was a ring of the door-bell. The pizzas had arrived.

They sat and munched.

'This is the vegetarian one, is it?' Sylvie asked, suspicious.

'Don't think there's much of any substance in either of them, to be honest. They make them out of some sort of technicolour straw. Doubt any living creature has ever been near either yours or mine, apart from the bloke on the moped who just did the delivery, and I'm not entirely convinced about his credentials as a form of organic life either, if we're getting technical. Shouldn't worry about it if I were you. Have another glass of wine.'

Take-away pizza and chianti in large crystal glasses. Sylvie chewed distractedly and looked at the image from the *Vollard Suite* she was sitting before. The minotaur was a tangle, knotted in the threads of his own baffling desire. And this tangle mingled with the other tangle that was the woman; the tangle of her hair, cranial and pubic, the tangle of her own insides, of her children yet to be born, their dark knotted lifelines. Sylvie chewed and looked.

'Worked it all out yet?' he asked, without taking his eyes off another of the prints.

'No.'

This was the chapter 'Labyrinth' in *Afterlife of the Image*. This was what had originally brought her out here. She sometimes wondered if it might be what still did. And Henry occasionally wondered the same thing.

'Lascaux. Chauvet.'

'Altamira.'

'Those figures, what are they called again?'

'Therianthropes.'

'Remind me.'

'Part man, part animal.'

'Like the minotaur.'

'Like the minotaur. Also like shamans, who dress up with headgear representing an animal.'

'And Goya.'

'The Black Paintings. Locked up in his house, curtains drawn, painting directly on the walls. Creatures of preternatural power.'

'Like therianthropes.'

'Maybe.'

'The craving to make and see images in the dark.'

'Picasso painted through the night.'

'And then see them in some sort of ritual. Like going to the cinema and waiting for the lights to go down, is that what you're saying? Or watching Dylan up on stage: wasn't he another of your images?'

'He was Hamlet dressed in black, telling all the merrymakers to stop making merry. And Lennon: don't forget Lennon. My paper on the iconography of the Beatles for the Institute got me into all this in the first place. Went down well in Liverpool.'

'Why them?'

'Because they really got started underground, in a place called The Cavern, wearing those animal skins we call leather jackets, and because when Brian Epstein was stopped dead on the pavement outside, it wasn't because the sound they were making was more sophisticated than the ones he'd heard before, but because it was more primitive. I suppose primitive here means finding and expressing a form. Primitive means escaping what Brancusi said realism had become by the beginning of the twentieth century: "a confusion of familiarities". It was what primitivism offered to artistic form that led Picasso to these shapes on your walls.'

'But how can you ever tie all thus stuff together?'

'I can't as yet. That's why the book stays unfinished. But I think you'll find, when it does get tied, that it will be through lenses and constellations.'

'Which lenses did your man from the Upper Palaeolithic use then?' She put down her glass, and pointed both her index fingers, one to the left eye, one to the right.

'And are we in the labyrinth here then?'

'Certainly looks that way from the images on your walls, Henry.'

'The Riverside Gallery. Home of the Shropshire minotaur. Featuring the famous Knossos take-away pizza.'

'And there must have been the odd boatload of virgins brought here to sate your appetites, surely.'

'I fear you exaggerate.'

'Maybe at least an occasional evening of rumpy-pumpy with a local Shrewsbury slapper?' Henry put down his glass and looked grave.

'There are no slappers in Shrewsbury, my dear. All the womenfolk about these parts are fragrant and cultured, little Mary Archers one and all, but without the vulgarity of the attendant husband.' By now Sylvie had finished all she could eat of the pizza, and was concentrating on her wine. It was very nice; no one could fault Henry's taste in wine. But what about his taste in women?

'Don't mind me asking, Henry, but you did say you'd been married three times.'

'I had three very successful marriages, yes.'

'What's that like? I mean, I've only ever done it once, and I find myself getting curious as to what the experience might be like on the occasion of a repeat performance. Does it get any easier?'

Henry had now finished his pizza, and re-filled his glass from the bottle. He held the bottle up beckoningly, but Sylvie shook her head. Never could keep up with Henry's intake.

'I wouldn't say easier, no. It's probably a bit like parachute-jumping: you grow more aware of the perils each time you do it, but that doesn't necessarily stop you. I'm not sure I'd trust memory here, if I were you. I certainly don't. But let's be chronological. My first wife and I were completely unsuited. But neither of us were to know that at the time, were we? She worked in one of those high-rise offices, where money sub-divides itself into fresh-faced zeros; it was a sort of high-tech perch, and she was a raptor surveying the bright new world below. They called it London in those days. She was so efficient that by the end I felt I couldn't even sleep in her presence without provoking her to fury. She would explain to me in the morning how untidily I slept, how raggedly I dreamed, what a noisy somnambulist I'd become, grunting and groaning and casting all the sheets around.'

'Like a minotaur.'

'Like a minotaur, staying over in the guest room of a convent. They're famously light sleepers, particularly when there are virgins around.

'By the end even her cooking seemed to reproach me. She'd serve up these perfect little lasagnes, with a sprig of the neatest herb you've ever seen. Fennel, I seem to recall, straight out of the culinary clinic. Swiss greenery. The cleanest of all possible greens. I felt the meals should be eating me rather than the other way round. Lovemaking was similarly tidy, strictly time-tabled. *Try not to make too much noise, Henry. This is a terraced house, after all. Can't you stay in one place for more than ten seconds, for heaven's sake?'*

'So you got divorced.'

'Yes, that was very neat too, if recollection serves.'

'What happened next?'

'What happened next was Laura. Ah Laura. Mad as a bloody hatter.' He took a deep drink of his wine for solace, and smiled briefly at the absurdity of life. His own and, if she was reading him aright, everyone else's too.

'So what attracted you then?'

'Erotomania, that's what. There were two Lauras; one in bed, one out. The one on the mattress could make you forget the other one for hours at a time, even days. Years of training as a trumpet-player meant that she had developed a particular gift for *embouchement* . . . But forgive me, I didn't mean to become indelicate . . . '

Play your cards right and you might have a trip down memory lane later, Sylvie thought. She felt, to borrow a phrase, that she owed him one.

'So was that the marriage that ended badly?'

'No, I seem to recall it ended rather well. It was the beginning and the middle bits that were awful. Eighteen months of non-communication, punctuated by bouts of uncontrolled Dionysian frenzy on our lavender silk sheets. Still, it could have been worse. She might still be here.'

Instead of me, Sylvie thought.

'And the last one?'

'The last one was Eleanor, God bless her. A lovely woman, who gave me all this. All this and more.' Henry faltered. For the first time, she sensed some real pain beneath the seeming insouciance.

'Not tempted by misogamy then, Henry?'

'Might be, if I knew what it was.'

'Detestation of the honourable estate of matrimony.'

'No, not at all. Not sure how soon I'll be doing it again myself, you know, but I wouldn't want to put anyone else off. One of life's intriguing journeys. Might you be planning another little trip, by any chance?'

The journey down into the delta, she heard herself saying silently, without really thinking it. Owen's terminology, that. Go away, Owen. Two things never failed Owen, however often his memory did: his words and his prick.

Later they stood in front of the image of the minotaur blinded, and being led away by the girl with the shining face. Ten minutes later, Henry undressed her lovingly, but she couldn't escape the notion that he might be close to tears. This seemed to happen whenever Eleanor was mentioned. Even as he made love to her, she could sense them maybe welling up behind his eyes. It was touching in a way. He couldn't escape his memories, could he, any more than she could escape hers? Afterlives. Maybe they should both book some amnesia lessons with Owen. How to forget Eleanor; how to forget Owen. Owen Treadle: Purveyor of the Waters of Lethe. Therapeutic treatments. By Appointment Only. Let's kill the afterlife of the image, folks.

Murmuring, sighing, barking, thumping. He was struggling somewhere in the empty corridor of his dream, this minotaur to whom she had been delivered, and he had woken her. She couldn't bear it, his hairy entanglement in the filaments of his own desire, past and present. How many dead wives was he clawing away at over there? And had it been any better while they'd been live wives? He thrashed at the pillows.

Pugilistic, demented. She began to see his first wife's point: Henry was a seriously untidy dreamer. She only stayed all night occasionally. And so she put her arms around him, turned him round gently, coaxed him. Felt the full weight of his bull belly upon her. By the time he arrived inside her, he was barely awake, but quelled now all the same, the riddle in his body and his mind solved, however momentarily, as he slumped back into a silent sleep, limbs flung uselessly about her. And once he'd slipped back down his foxhole, Sylvie herself started to weep. Silently and very gently. *Lachrymosa.* Looks like our evening has been themed, Henry, with pizzas and tears, and now I've been left to do all the blubbing for both of us. Outside, the rain was an animal, desperate to get back inside the earth, its myriad puny horns demanding entrance. She knew that the rain would enter Henry's dream, swelling the mighty river of discontent inside him, and drowning whatever it encountered.

Wolf Morning

Owen had driven back from the coast. How that car of his throttled and howled. He had woken with a hunger that had no memory attached to it; a primeval hunger that had never before tasted food. An appetite innocent of everything except its own brute force. He had asked for two breakfasts, one after the other. He had tried to make a joke of this with the landlady, and had smiled his winning smile, dark eyes glinting with mischief, but she had not smiled back. Instead she had looked at him as though she knew something dark about him that he might not know himself. Something darker than either his hair or his eyes. Something that cancelled his smile. The word Alex might have entered his mind momentarily then, but he wouldn't let it in. He still had a gift for closing his mind, when required. Sylvie knew that, well enough.

He parked the car outside the house and went in. After making himself a coffee he found the shelf Sylvie had mentioned. He looked along the titles. These were his works, weren't they? The television films he had made with Johnny Tamworth, the films he wrote and Johnny directed, and yet he would be surprised by them, all the same. Some videos, some DVDs. Down in the cellar there were film cans. He remembered.

Loving Every Minute. Five minutes later he was sitting in an armchair with a coffee in his hand, staring at the television screen. The opening of the film stretched out one single take, like a tightrope of gum that wouldn't snap, however far it pulled from the teeth that held it. Pupil of the right eye zooming out in millimetres to take in brow, forehead, cheek (a woman, then), glass, table, torso (a woman finely modelled, well-endowed), bar, crowd (to whose haphazard constellation inside the solitary cell of thought she seemed no more related than a fly to the pattern of the wallpaper it traverses). And all the while the voice, low, sardonic, cracked, charged equally with eroticism and melancholy, speaks in monotones, equable and despairing. I created her, Owen thought. Am I God, then? Listen as she speaks, my creature.

'I remember the day well because it was my birthday. It was also the first time my husband ever hit me. And, to be honest, I was glad of the attention: it had been a long time since he'd concentrated so forcibly on his wife. For years what I had done, what I had been, had not been important enough for him to lash out like that. I hadn't deserved so much expenditure of his precious energy. Even as I nursed the bruise, anaesthetizing it with another large whisky (and how many did that make on this particular day?) I congratulated myself on once more holding him inside my little circle of light.

'A woman doesn't want to focus a man on her profile; she wants to blind him with her dazzle, believe me. Blind, in chains, how mightily the fellow rattles. Close the cage door then and lock it, a cage woven from earthshine and grief. You have a key in your hand now.'

And the shot, like the universe itself if gravity should prove powerful enough, than the repellent forces, has stopped expanding, the gum was rewinding again into its chewing maw, and Owen reversed with it, space contracting, but this time not to the eye, which swallowed its photons, but to the mouth, which swallowed its prey. The mouth to which the large whisky had now been lifted and gulped, greedily, to the chimes of the ice cubes. Red lipsticked mouth, fleshy, ornate. A gratuitous sign. The music began then like an obscenity, a tempo of swagger and swank, and he saw the man's back as he moved into camera. All you could see of him was the strength of his back, and the compliance of her gaze raised to meet him.

Owen knew that if he had to see any more he'd pass out, and he switched the set off. He had created that. But why?

*

When you make an image you leave the world. That's what Sylvie had come to believe and that was the answer to Henry's question, 'How can you bring it all together?' Lenses and constellations. The labyrinth, the caves at Lascaux and Chauvet, Goya's black paintings, Picasso's minotaur. Make an image, leave the world. Leave it by re-shaping it as your own. We look out there and see constellations. Of recurrence and desire. Sometimes of the recurrence of desire.

Deep down in those caves she reckoned there was only one thing we could be absolutely sure of: there were never any ibex or aurochs or bison around. Whether our ancestors from the Upper Palaeolithic were in a trance-state or not when they created those figures, they had taken away the image from the point of its perception, since the image was being created without any creature before them. And once we'd managed that mighty leap, to separate the image from its origin in perception, then we were condemned to carry the world around inside our heads. It grew heavier and heavier, our precious reliquary, filled as it was with so many sacred images. She was now on the A483. In twenty minutes time she'd be in Chester. Hardly any traffic.

At the end of a mile of an anthracite-black, constrictingly narrow passageway, you find the image of a woolly mammoth. He had certainly never come down here, now had he? He couldn't have even fitted through the passageway. But his image had now survived the creature's extinction. The afterlife of images. How would she explain it to them in her lecture that evening? She needed to get home and change out of her short dress and black stockings. Go from black-stocking to blue-stocking. A little bit of a queue up ahead. The roundabout.

How about manoeuvring around it like this? In the mouth of a cave stands one of those hominids whom we call prehistoric. Living, that is, before history and written records begin. Such bones might speak to us, should we ever find them, but nothing else will, except for the marks the creature has made on stone. Should some unforeseen miracle of science and technology bring our cave creature back to life, we might even hear the noises that once emerged from her larynx, but we wouldn't understand them. She stares out now at the night sky. She sees a shape, a form that comes into being if you join up the lights in the sky with your own eyes. And she remembers. She saw such a shape in that same corner of the sky the last time it was as cold as this, the last time it grew dark before they could find their prey, the last time leaves fell so wetly on her face. So it's a shape that returns then. Not only in the sky but in the mind, where it is now fast transmuting to a tree, a fish, a creature of the forest. Constellations.

I will tell them, she thinks, how this is a speculative moment, even if a highly possible one. If I can just clear that roundabout I'll be through it. This might be the furthest we can go back in time through the development of our species to find the extremities of perception. It is an edge not only because our prehistoric man is here seeing the furthermost object in his universe, a signal sent from the edge of our reality, both in space and time; nor because this represents a boundary where we might find the origins of the patterned world we created and create, where we endlessly orienteer ourselves towards the existence that surrounds and engulfs us. It is also an edge because this is where perception begins. Before, there was a world of sentience and instinct, but now we have perceptions, which depend on memory for their function, and images for their representation. If a perception is to separate itself from the sentient flux, it must form a memorable shape; it must recur, if only in consciousness. In one manoeuvre we have given birth to perception, memory and the image. And in the process what we have created is the first constellation.

I want you all to think for a moment about what it means to constellate. To fill the heavens with ploughs and goddesses and horses. What's interesting is that the shapes are both there and not there. We join up the dots in our minds; we relate stars and planets which are otherwise unrelated except by the weakest of the four forces controlling our world: gravity. In populating the skies with creatures both real and mythic, with implements that can't be too much use for ploughing all that inter-stellar dust, we are engaging in both science and art, since this is what they both ultimately do: constellate data into meaningful shapes and recurrent patterns. We make images, and then we can't escape them. They take over reality in the process of defining it. Our early woman in the cave-mouth has arrived at art's first moment, and science's too. Now she can no longer tell the image from the stars, and she never will again. She has become fully human. Poor bitch.

Sylvie pulled up outside the house behind Owen's car. She climbed out and ran her hand along the bonnet, the long sleek Morgan bonnet. It was still warm from its recent accelerations. He couldn't have been back long then. She couldn't face going in. For tonight the blue-stocking would have to be a black-stocking. She'd better remember not to cross her legs. Lionel already found it difficult to concentrate on her lectures as it was.

*

Owen had been making mental lists of things he couldn't remember the taste of: treacle, porridge, taramasalata, cauliflower, haddock, guacamole, cocoa and beer. He wanted to taste them all quickly. The words already had their own tastes on his tongue. He would go and get some beer now, and that would be one of them at least ticked off the list. He left the house and stopped at the first pub he came to.

'Beer please.'

'Which one?' the barman asked, and gestured at the array of his pumps. Owen pointed to the sign nearest the barman's elbow.

'That's a good beer.'

'Excellent. Because that's what I really need now. A good beer.'

'Been a long time, has it ?

'Seems like a lifetime.'

As the barman pulled his pint, he resumed his conversation with the melancholy figure slouched over the bar. This fellow was in a grey tracksuit, but it didn't look as though he'd been doing much running lately.

'So what happened, Col?' The melancholy figure took a drink of his beer and sighed.

'Why can't women understand that men don't like shopping? Can you tell me that, Dave?'

'It's a mystery.'

'It's a fucking mystery. Anyway, I was trying to escape having to go shopping that Saturday with the wife by going in to work instead. So it actually suited me to tell the secretary that she'd have to go in and do the work she'd missed out on by her absence. By the time I turned up that Saturday afternoon, her ladyship was already there, wasn't she, catching up on her admin with a certain amount of . . . what's the word I'm looking for now?'

'Displeasure?'

'That'll have to do.'

' "Hello Dot," I said.'

'Dot. That was my mother's name.'

'Well I sincerely hope the similarities end there, Dave. Dot did not reply at first but just carried on thwacking these green card files one against another. So I persevered. After all, I was the manager in those days, remember. "I said, Hello Dot."'

This last statement, Owen noted, was issued in a raised voice, with a faint hint of menace. Now the voice quavered into a tremolo as Colin imitated Dot: '"You always had it in for me," she said. I was taken aback, to be honest. "I did not," I said. "At the beginning I was very fond of you." Now see how I walked into the trap, Dave.' His voice once more trilled to drag-queen proportions. ' "There you are. *At the beginning.* Not any more though." I was convinced she was going to cry. Can't stand women blubbing.'

'Tricky.'

'I'll have a re-fill, I think. Thirsty work remembering all this. Anyway she's still on her knees, isn't she, banging away at her bloody filing. Always wore this white blouse with the tight bit round the throat.'

'Choker.'

'That's it. White blouse and purple brassiere. No good pretending you didn't notice it. I mean, it was all designed to be noticed, wasn't it? I'd inherited her from the previous manager, and I reckon he'd been giving her one. Certainly didn't take her on for her typing speed or telephone manner, that's for sure. So muggins here starts feeling guilty. And I couldn't take my eyes off her back. There was a bit of loose silk showing just above the skirt.'

'That would have been a slip.'

'Don't get many of those these days, do you? For some reason.

Hardly an essential item of clothing for the practical business-woman, I'd say: worn primarily for provocation. Anyway I decide to pour oil on troubled waters. So what do I say? "I'm very fond of you actually, Dot." Now what's interesting about that remark, Dave, looking back on it from this vantage-point in time, is that it's completely untrue. I never could stand the stuck-up, hoity-toity fucking cow from the first moment I set eyes on her.'

'You were trying to be diplomatic, Colin.'

'Exactly.' Colin's voice rose an octave once more. ' "You're very fond of me? Is that true, Colin?" So I nodded, thinking I'd resolved a problematic situation in the office. And before I know where I am she's fleetfooted it across the carpet and she's giving me a tongue sarny.'

'Oops.'

'Not just that. Before I have an opportunity to . . . to . . . '

'Collect your thoughts?'

'Collect my thoughts, her hand swishes down the inside of my tracksuit bottoms. And believe me, Dave, the girl knew what she was doing, if you know what I mean. She knew which bits of a man's anatomy to press, and in what order. Not her first encounter with a fellow's tackle, I'd have said. I mean, it was a difficult situation for any bloke to extricate himself from.'

'And you in a managerial role, of course.'

'And me in a managerial role. "God, Dot," I said, or something like that. I wasn't exactly keeping a diary of events at the time.'

'She should have been doing that, surely?'

'How do you mean?'

'Diarising events: it's a secretarial job.'

'Gotcha. "I've always like you, Col." The imitated voice now achieved a register of near-strangulation. ' "You should have given me some sort of sign." '

'And what did you say?'

'What did I say? *Aaarghhh*. Or something like that. You don't always choose your words all that fastidiously on these occasions, let's be honest. I suppose I might have expressed some surprise at this sudden turn of events, but by now . . . ' Colin halted and took a deep drink of his beer.

'Things were going from bad to worse, eh?'

'I think, looking back on it with the benefit of hindsight, I might have pointed out to Dotty that we were obviously lurching from one extreme to another, in terms of staff relations, but she'd have had a bit of a problem answering by then.'

'Oh? Why's that then?'

'Because her mouth was full.'

'Ah. Point of no return now reached, by the sound of it.'

'Not what you'd call a practical staff assessment moment.'

'Sounds like she was assessing your staff practically enough.'

'It was all over in a couple of minutes – I mean, it hadn't been planned. Or at least, I don't think it had. The secretary handed me a Kleenex tissue, and left, saying she might do a bit more filing on the Monday, if she felt like it; but on the other hand, she might not. And that was the first time I'd looked through the window. On the rooftop opposite there's these two blokes in yellow helmets. They gave me the thumbs-up sign and a big cheer.'

'Weekend workers, one and all, I suppose. Sense of solidarity.'

'Trouble is, they went round blabbing about it, didn't they? Finally the boss got to hear. Most put out, he was. Said I was turning his offices into a brothel. So I ended up getting the sack.'

'And now your wife's left you as well.'

'And now my fucking wife's left me as well.'

'Might have been easier to just to go shopping that Saturday, Col.'

'That's what I'll do next time. Definitely.'

'Supermarkets have been getting more user-friendly.'

Owen had now finished his beer. Another hole had been filled in his mind, and he left.

The Convenience of Women

Henry Allardyce was considering Picasso and his women. It was twelve o'clock and Henry wished that it were already one, because then he could pour himself a glass of wine. But rules were rules. No wine before one. Picasso's imagination and his art fed upon women, that was for sure. His style changed irrevocably every time a new one arrived and an old one departed.

There was Fernande Olivier, whose slow heavy-fleshed carnality he celebrated asleep and awake, drawing her making love or merely existing inside the ruinous state of domesticity to which their life together soon reduced them. Even Picasso's friends were shocked at the shambles they inhabited, and some of those friends lived in sufficiently insalubrious rat-holes themselves. When she started to become ill he told his friends she'd turned into a machine for suffering. To make Picasso jealous, she beckoned others between the sheets. It worked: it did make him jealous. Sadly it also made him hate her.

Little Eva he obviously loved, and she managed to die of the malignant growths inside her before he was provided with a single serious chance to change his mind.

Olga, the Russian ballet virgin, was the first one he had to marry to possess. Even in the portraits he painted of her, many in the style of Ingres, you can see what she was: an effigy of proprietorial self-importance. She actually managed to turn Picasso into a stiff, self-preening bourgeois, though fortunately not for ever.

Dora Maar, that chameleon soul who was greatly gifted herself, let her identity be made over from profligate anguish to the dedicated anguish of being Pablo's lover and she never recovered. Picasso called her the most convenient woman he'd ever met – if you wanted her to be a dog, she was a dog, if a bird, a bird, if a cloud, well then a cloud. She could even be an abstract notion or a year gone by or a thunderstorm. She would scream at him in her rages, only to beg forgiveness afterwards and say she would once more be anything, anyone, anywhere he chose to specify. She had stepped straight out of Ovid, ready to change shape into tree or wind, except that she didn't shift forms to escape a god, but to embrace one, to bring him back into her mind and flesh, to have him home again inside her thoughts, between her legs. Later, long after Pablo had gone, she returned to the practice of Catholicism. Her observance by the end of her life was as strict as a nun's. The little god from Spain had been replaced by the big one from the sky.

Marie-Thérèse Walter was no more than a schoolgirl when he met her. She adored him. He didn't so much re-create as create her. For years his painting rejoiced in the curvature of womanhood and the bright colours of fecundity. It was an incestuous relationship with a new little sister. He left her but she never left him. Even after he'd finished with her he remained the centre of her life till the end of her days. Not long after he died she committed suicide by taking poison. And she was the figure in so many of the etchings from the *Vollard Suite*.

Françoise Gilot was the only one who actually walked out on him. That was a first and he made sure there was no repeat performance.

Then the faithful Jacqueline saw him through to the end.

Change a woman, change a life. That seemed to be Picasso's motto. The question now was this: had this happened to Henry too? In some ways, it undoubtedly had. Now: was it about to happen again? Break the rules, Henry. There was no one in the gallery. He went through to the kitchen and poured himself a glass of *Nuits St George*. He wanted something decent to help him think. 12.30 is in any case so close to one o'clock as makes no difference.

His insouciant account of his marriages in fact covered several wounds, as Sylvie had suspected. His first marriage drew to a conclusion with great rapidity when it became evident to Henry that his wife had been conducting an affair for over a year with one of her business partners, a much neater and richer man than Henry had been at the time. Or was now, or ever would be, if it came to that. He could still remember how he had lain awake in his bed and raged, cuckold hours transmuting into eunuch days. He felt as though he had been living in the harem of another man's pleasures. By then, the only thing unveiled for him each night was the spectre of his own humiliation. Laura had simply come and gone, leaving him sore in the process, but Eleanor. Poor Eleanor. As he sipped at his premature glass of wine, he turned the pages of his address book until he found Sylvie's number at the Institute. He had her mobile too but he didn't want to talk to her now, only to leave a message.

'This is the minotaur. Now you know that I won't eat you, will you be coming back again before long? I've been tidying the labyrinth in anticipation.'

As the call was being recorded at the Institute, it was picked up by Hamish Flyte on his RECE monitoring system. He grabbed the phone immediately and dialled 1471 before another call could come in. He then phoned the number provided.

'Riverside Gallery. How may I help you?' Hamish now adopted his wheedling tone.

'Sorry. So sorry. Could I just ask who I'm speaking to?'

'Henry Allardyce.'

'Now I *am* getting confused. Would there be anyone else at the gallery?'

'No, I'm the only one here.'

'Thank you. I think I must definitely have got a wrong number.' He put down the phone and made a note of Henry's name.

When he heard the keys clinking against Sylvie's door later in the afternoon, he quickly opened his own.

'Hello there. What a lovely outfit. Delightful little black skirt, Sylvie. You look as though you're on your way to a date; or coming back from one, perhaps. How's your work in the labyrinth going?'

'*In* the labyrinth, Hamish? You mean on the labyrinth, presumably.' She was laughing. Silly little man.

'Oh, do I?'

She didn't have time to listen to her messages, but gathered together her notes and went straight to the lecture theatre. It was full. That was gratifying. Lionel fixed his eyes on her legs, where they remained for the following fifty minutes.

'I want to start with a quote from the poet W. B. Yeats. He is thinking of the goings-on in séances, in which he was very interested. The emanation of spirits. Ectoplasm. Here's what he says: "If photographs that I saw handed round in Paris thirty years ago can be repeated and mental images photographed, the distinction that Berkeley drew between what man creates and what God creates will have broken down." Now just think about this for a moment. Photographs are going to abolish the distinction between what man creates and what God creates. Photographs. The afterlife of images. Conan Doyle had already become convinced of something similar, when he believed those photographs of the Cottingley Fairies. They were fakes, of course, but they fooled the creator of Sherlock

Holmes, that fool-proof detective. Why such an extraordinary dependence on the photograph? Might it be because of our distrust of the human imagination? Might it be because we wish to make memory scientific, and therefore forensically irrefutable? Might it be because we have so come to distrust our own eyes that we wish only to trust the cyclopean eye of our recording lenses? That way we can separate the image from all subjectivity. This would explain a great deal of the modern cult of celebrity, since only those who spend enough time before the cyclopean eye can be said to be truly alive. Until you are sufficiently photographed, you haven't even been born. This might be one explanation why people are prepared to abandon all their dignity for the sake of ten minutes on a television programme. Because they have now been made immortal in an image. We're all Egyptian pharaohs now. The painted food on our walls is an image, so it can never rot. That's the origin of the still life. Anyway, next week we are going to examine photographs from the cave at Lascaux. Let's see if we can work out how every single image appears to have been painted by Picasso.'

She had at some point, without thinking, moved around to the front of the table and sat down on it, crossing her legs. She always did this. But she didn't usually wear the short black skirt and stockings she'd chosen for Henry the previous night. Alison came up to her afterwards with a wary smile – she was merely fulfilling the University's peer-review requirements by attending the lecture in the first place.

'Decided to promote your talks amongst the male student body, I see, Sylvie?'

'Why?'

'It's just, with that skirt, if a chap had been in the right place this evening, he could have caught the whites of your thighs above the stocking-tops. I did.'

'Oh shit.'

'Lionel's gone off in search of para-medical attention. Or maybe just a bar. I've been told that alcohol in sufficient quantities produces detumescence.'

Only when she got back to her room did she listen finally to the message from Henry. Minotaur. It struck her what Hamish had said earlier. In the labyrinth. Coming to or from a date. There had been a rumour for some time that Hamish listened in on everyone's calls, keeping personal files on the lot of them. This caused some merriment; some irritation. Nobody was sure if it was legal under the new European legislation. She felt no merriment at all, but considerable irritation. She walked across the corridor to his room and, after the most perfunctory of knocks, walked in.

'Hamish, have you been listening to my calls?'

'I have to monitor all calls to the Institute; it's done on a strictly one-in-X random-selection principle.'

'Well, I'd appreciate it if, in future, one-in-X is someone else and not me. Because I don't like it.'

'Goodness. You do seem to be making a habit of taking the bull by the horns at the moment.'

'Not sure about that, Hamish. But I've always been very good at taking the Jock by the jockstrap. And I once saw a farm demonstration: how to turn a bull into a bullock. So watch it.'

Then as she was turning away, he said this: 'Oh, by the way. Your husband phoned this morning. He wondered if you might be here, since you apparently weren't there. Sadly not, I told him. I had no idea of your whereabouts, of course, any more than he did.'

Sylvie drove through the Birkenhead Tunnel in a state of chilled exasperation. No graffiti down here, she noticed. Even the taggers weren't prepared to endure so much carbon monoxide for their urban art. She put on the cassette that her best student had given her the day before. Paul Darcy. *Through the Concrete Corridors*. 'He's into some of the same things you are,' the student had said. She tried to concentrate on the music and ignore the hundred thousand tons of water thrashing about above her.

> *Dreams and speculations, fragments washed up by the waves*
> *Ruins under mountains and ancient treasures deep in caves*
> *I stepped into your labyrinth, I heard the monster roar*
> *But a doctor in a white coat with a clipboard led me gently*
>   *to the door*
> *And when you arrived with a pen-torch and a smile on*
>   *your face*
> *Bringing all the medicine I'd need for my stay in this place*
> *Through the concrete corridors, your smiling words were*
>   *feathery and slight*
> *When the blindfold came off, darkness flashed not light.*

Another minotaur, then. Blinded by passion and bewilderment. But she couldn't concentrate, and switched over to the news instead. More slaughter in the caverns there. Bombs going off in the mountains. When she arrived back she heard the sound of one of Johnny and Owen's films. She walked across to the set and switched the sound off.

'Why did you phone the Institute this morning?'

'To find out where you were . . . how you were.'

'How very solicitous. You bugger off to Llandudno and then start snooping around after me.'

'I wasn't snooping. Anyway, where were you?'

'With a friend.'

'Have a name, this friend?

'I don't owe you anything, Owen. I'm not saying you owe me anything either, but I definitely don't owe you anything.'

'Do you want a coffee?'

'Yes, please. I'll go have a shower and get changed.'

'I like the get-up, to be honest. Only hope your friend did.'

Then he went to the kitchen. She turned and looked at the silent images on the screen. Torn posters on a decaying wall. Balls of dead grass blowing down the street. A child crouched beside a blown-up truck, his face a miniature diagram of the world's desolation.

'Do you want me to sleep in the other room again?'

'Yes please.'

But he came to bed anyway, half an hour after her. Lay beside her. Placed a hand on her breast.

'No.'

'It was so warm the other night.'

'So warm you went to Llandudno the following day. It had been a long time before that, Owen. Given everything that had happened. Maybe you haven't remembered it all yet. Alex, I mean.'

He hadn't removed his hand; neither had she.

'I was just trying to help you remember who you were. So much of sex is politeness, remember. A woman in one of your scripts says that.'

Only minutes before falling asleep did she remember Henry. She hadn't phoned him back. He'd survive the night though, wouldn't he?

Earth, Water, Fire and Air

Alex read the passage from *The One True Elemental* for the fourth time and told herself that the pain in her gut was merely the sound of earthly grossness leaving. So much corruption for so long had rotted the invisible conduits and made them flesh-like in weightiness and sloth. She was being pulled down temporarily towards what Lady Pneuma called the dark plumbing of sad bodies, the potbellies, the grosstongues, those with soulless skins and iron brains. The pain was the low dirge of lament of a defeated army stumbling home. Soon enough she would hit the wall of elation, that resurrection into the region of Mary's colour, the azure of the abandonment of the fleshly. Pneuma had described it so beautifully. It would soon be hers. Only for now the pain, the sweats, the cramps and the cold. Such a terrible cold. She had never felt so shiveringly cold; the soul itself seemed to shiver. Shaking off the filth of its imprisonment. That was the dark matter leaving.

She could still just manage to turn around and see the image of Pneuma, a vague vignette, framed in a white-heart plastic frame, redolent of sainthood. It made her look considerably thinner than she actually was these days, but her skin was still lit from the light within. And she also saw Owen Treadle, whom she did not choose to see at all. His ectoplasmic face was grinning, pursuing her across space and time. 'Go on, you can do it. It's not really happening, Alex. This is acting, for God's sake.' But it was really happening, wasn't it? Even something only made to be re-played again and again on film still had to happen. Images could not have an afterlife unless they had a life first. She passed out then.

Lady Pneuma now claimed one hundred thousand members worldwide. There was no way of affirming or disproving this statement, since if she kept any records, she had not as yet made them available to anyone else. The Inland Revenue in Britain and the IRS in the States were both beginning to make some interested murmurs about all this. But Pneuma, while seemingly living at the Claymore for one half of the year, and the New York Waldorf for the other, remained elusive. Her communications with the world were carefully controlled. A DVD (Alex had it in her bag, but there was no way of playing it in the electricity-free bothie); occasional booklets; hermetic appearances on television, very infrequent, and controlled entirely by the Delta Foundation. Her followers had to turn back to the compacted wisdom brought together in the pages of *The One True Elemental*. There they could find it all. All that she had discovered. All she had endured. Everything she had now transcended.

Alex was clutching her copy, even as she sank into un-consciousness. Her own copy was signed; or at least the words Lady Pneuma had been imprinted on its title-page in some manner. A few sceptical journalists who had set off in pursuit of the enigmatic lady were far from convinced that she spent her days signing books for her numerous disciples. Alex had the special copy because, after paying three hundred pounds to become an associate member, she had then spent a further four hundred to become a full initiate. This accorded her privileges, like the signed book, in which she had read – enchantingly – that the urethra had only become so engrossed and enfleshed at a late stage in female evolution. Before that it had been a translucent passageway through which light could travel freely. This had been the burden of the myth of Zeus and Danae: though encased in her tower of flesh, Danae was penetrated by the luminous shower of gold. In other words, the riches of the world of light had overcome all obstacles and seeded the womb of the future. So what did gods live on and in? Air, of course. Like Pneuma herself.

Alex had also been entitled as a full initiate to personal communication with Lady Pneuma; this prospect had been what had prompted her to spend the extra money. In her desperation before leaving to head north the month before, she had phoned and phoned. Day after day after day. Over a hundred times. But it was always the same recorded message she found herself listening to.

'This is Lady Pneuma. You are now a full initiate of the Delta Foundation, which has found the path of escape from a life of bodily entrapment. We are free spirits who live only on what the spirit offers. If you have not made the full journey yet, you must understand that you now have the means to do so. I have eaten nothing but air for ten years. Take a look at my pictures . . . '

The Second Interval

Henry Allardyce looked in the mirror. He couldn't really blame Sylvie for not phoning back; he wouldn't have phoned himself back, if he'd been a woman. God, look at yourself, Allardyce. Your hair needs cutting. You haven't bothered shaving. Your shirt collar is frayed. Your doctor says your blood-pressure is always on the up and up. Where's it all going to end?

Phttt, he thought. I'll go like that. Run out of air one day like a dead balloon. *Phttt*. Shrivelled skin on the pavement where the boots go hurrying by. One great *phttt*, and a mild, baffled obit in the local paper. Heading for flame and ashes, and maybe a little earthenware vase with a name inscribed and two dates: from this terminus to that one. A life. The exit from the womb and the entry to the grave. And as for the rest, the civic amenity site or, as we used to say when syllables were rationed during the war, the tip. Not my Picassos though; not my minotaurs. No one will be chucking those away. And, pray, what do you do about it all, sir? Pour yourself another glass of wine and listen to Thelonius Monk, why don't you?

Monk was a particular favourite of Henry's, who liked a great deal of modern jazz before it decided to abandon the tune entirely, though he had been told it had recently been returning home to it. Monk's version of *Nice Work if you Can Get It* was plinking and plonking through the gallery at the moment, gathering up contingencies as it went and transmuting each one into own weird causality. Henry poured himself a glass of red. French *vin de table*. Nothing fancy. Mustn't spend too much this month. Then the bell rang to indicate that someone had entered. Henry took a stern swig of his glass, adopted an expression of entirely insincere affability, and walked through to the main room. It was Bernard Trasker, MBE and Mrs Bernard Trasker, MBE by gender proxy and adoption. Henry could never think of them as anything other than this, since Bernard seldom let an opportunity pass of telling everyone about the existence of his gong. It was all over his letterhead, his compliment slips. Even, Henry suspected, his notes to the milkman. Probably had it embroidered on his socks. Should he ever omit to mention the honour, his wife would make good the lacuna. Her role as dutiful companion to a distinguished lifelong civil servant surely deserved some sort of recognition from the world. Bernard occasionally bought paintings for his fine old house up on the hill. Whatever he bought, his wife would disapprove of. She was looking with considerable disapproval now at the Nolan portrait of Rimbaud, which Bernard had been examining for the sixth or seventh time. Evidently pondering.

'Hello Henry.'

'Hello Bernard. Still thinking about the Nolan then?'

'It's a powerful piece of work.'

'But where on earth would it go, Bernie?' his wife asked. 'We can hardly have it in the front room. The man looks positively demented.'

'He has shuffled off the coils of civilisation,' Henry said.

'Well he might have kept one or two on, if only for decency's sake.'

'He has got down to the essential core of things,' Henry said, now in his curatorial role. He could prattle on merrily like this for hours. 'He is a poor, bare, forked creature. As are we all, up on the heath, if old King Lear is to be believed.' Mrs Bernard

79

Trasker MBE gave Henry a look of severely disapproving incomprehension.

'It would have to hang in my study. Then it wouldn't need to bother you, would it dear?'

'Awful lot of money for something that's only ever going to hang on the wall of your study.'

Henry was in a dilemma. He badly wanted to get back to his wine, but couldn't really go and get it without offering his potential clients one as well. He also needed to sell that painting. He decided on a strategy.

'Can I offer you both some red wine? Sadly, it's pretty ropey stuff. Cheap French plonk, but until I manage to sell one of these paintings here, I'm afraid it's all I can afford for the moment.' He hoped two birds might be slain with this one stone.

'No thank you,' said Mrs Bernard Trasker firmly.

'Very good of you, Henry. Don't mind if I do.'

As Henry went to fetch the wine, Mrs Trasker found herself listening to the music. When the gallery owner returned, she fixed her stare on him once more. He knew that stare. It was a stare that existed even when not attached to Mrs Bernard Trasker.

'He's playing the wrong notes, that piano player.'

'No,' Henry said evenly, 'he's playing the right notes. Your ears may not be accustomed to them. He is playing a lot of second intervals, where you're probably used to thirds, fifths and sevenths. But Monk himself said that there are no dissonances, only consonances we haven't got fully acquainted with yet. Schubert plays a fair number of second intervals in his *Sonata in B Flat Major*, but you've probably got used to them by now.

'Monk?'

'That's the piano player you're listening to. Thelonius Monk.'

'What a very odd name. Was that his real name?'

'I believe so, yes.'

'Can't imagine any of Bernie's colleagues in Whitehall with a name like that.'

'Thelonius Monk, OBE. No, it doesn't sound quite right does it?'

Bernard was still squinting admiringly at the Nolan. He was in fact a very knowledgeable collector. Henry found it utterly baffling that he could endure living with this wife of his for more than a day. Might she have brought money to the union? Could that have been her house at the top of the hill? Or was it possible that once upon a time she had been the most amazing fuck? Henry felt that the human imagination was in the process of reaching its limits here. Her suit was immaculately tailored, and she had evidently been to the hair-dresser's recently. Her hair had been dyed, and had now attained the texture of illuminated hay. It reminded him of those Knossos pizzas. Blinded minotaurs and beautiful women. The two men sipped at their wine, which wasn't all that bad, in fact. They'd both swigged worse in their time. Still, it was nothing like the *Chateau Neuf* he'd be returning to later.

'Tell Henry about Ludlow, Bernie,' Mrs Trasker said. Bernard was jolted from his reverie. 'Go on, tell him. You'll like this, Henry.' Bernard sighed, turned away from the Nolan, and proceeded.

'We'd gone down to Ludlow for the day. Even before we set off I had this pain in my thigh, but I get so many pains these days I decided to ignore it and while we walked round town, up and down the streets to the castle and what-have-you, I forgot all about the blessed pain. It was only when I was climbing into the car again that it hit me. But this time it had moved up to the . . . well, you know.' The two men looked at each other. They knew all right. What man doesn't?

'Right slap-bang in the middle of the whole caboodle. But by now it was so sharp, such a lethal stinging sensation that I suddenly knew what it had to be. I just knew it couldn't be anything else. The black proboscis of some malignant insect was injecting my tackle with its poison.' At this point Henry stopped drinking and put his glass down on the table. He stared at the other man with grave concentration. 'So I jumped back out of the car, unfastened my trousers and pulled down my underpants. There and then.' Mrs Trasker now interposed.

'I had to shout at him, "Bernard, have you gone barking mad? This isn't the beach at Tenerife." There was a poor woman crossing the car park with her shopping bags who turned tail there and then. Obviously thought she'd finally come face to face with the phantom Shropshire flasher. Dropping carrots out of her bag in her haste to be gone.'

'So what was it?' Henry asked.

'What was what?'

'This poisonous creature that had decided to make a meal of your . . . well, of you?'

'That was the extraordinary thing, you see,' Bernard said, turning up to the ceiling a mild look of philosophic distraction, the look of a veteran recalling distant battles, 'because it wasn't an insect at all. It was a needle.'

'A needle? What sort of needle?'

'Just an ordinary sewing needle. With its point a full half inch into my scrotum.' As if moved suddenly by the extent of the ordeal, Bernard walked back to the painting, put his half-moon spectacles on, and gave it a good long look. Henry picked up his wine glass and drained it. He stared at Mrs Trasker: 'I think you'll find in future that a small wax doll will normally serve just as well.'

Then the telephone rang. It was Sylvie.

'Excuse me,' Henry said, 'but I need to take this in the other room.' He went through to the kitchen and, with the handset crooked between his shoulder and his ear, he re-filled his glass.

'So how are you?'

'Confused Henry. I'm a very confused girl at the moment. You're not planning on confusing me any more, are you?' He knew exactly what she meant.

'Try not to.'

'We're friends who meet sometimes for a little comfort.'

'Don't leave it too long then, will you?'

'Did you by any chance get a caller with a Scots voice yesterday?' Henry thought for a moment.

'Yes, I did, funnily enough. It was a wrong number.'

'It wasn't actually. It was our Director of Studies, a grubby little schmuck called Hamish Flyte, who has taken to keeping records on us all for future use. All our little peccadilloes noted down.'

'Like a Chief Whip.'

'What do they do?'

'Keep tabs on everyone, dark notebooks filled with all your nastier moments, in case it all comes in handy for a bit of blackmail, when a division's looking iffy. But this isn't 1890. You're not breaking any laws, for God's sake.'

'I think he's just building up collateral. He reckons there might be a plot against him. He thinks we all hate him.'

'Why does he think that?'

'Because we all do. Nobody can even remember how he got in to the Institute; let alone how he ended up almost running it. He can still make the difference between grants and fellowships being renewed, all the same. Poisonous little toad. If he phones again, tell him to fuck off.'

'From both of us?'

'From both of us.'

'You could always come over and tell him yourself.' There

83

was a pause. 'When will you come and visit me again, Sylvie?'

'I don't know, love. If it's regular comfort you need, I think you should try out one of those fragrant Shrewsbury ladies.'

'Would it help if I turned vegetarian?'

'Wouldn't make much difference with those pizzas. You even said that yourself.'

*

Why vegetarian? The ancients believed in a homeopathic diet: if you want to be strong like a lion, then eat a lion; if lustful like a goat, eat goat. If you want to be cunning like the snake, cut the snake from its skin, cook it slowly with herbs and then consume it. To sing sweetly, swallow the nightingale before the song in its tiny throat starts congealing. To swim with savage grace, catch, roast and eat your shark. If you want to mock the gods and defecate in their sacred places, chew monkey in great quantities.

Now as for Sylvie, all she really wanted was to be as calm as a tree in the shade, quiet as grass in a storm, and so she had become a vegetarian. No blood would ever again pass her lips, not even the blood of the lamb. She reckoned slaughter's debris clogs the mind, making the spirit viscous and sluggish. It coarsens the delicate ganglia that connect us to time's wounds. And yet she was fascinated by Picasso, the least vegetarian of artists; he ate the world's flesh raw so as to make it his own. Ate years; became history. Swallowed ancient art, the flesh of unimaginable times and unimaginable minds, vivid traces of lost worlds, so as to become the one great primeval heir, Pablo, unquestionable Iberian son of the ages, erect in his cloak of flesh. Sylvie believed that her diet explained in part her equable temperament, though she didn't feel all that equable at the moment, if the truth were told. Work. She had some work to do. Constellations and lenses. Lecturing tomorrow.

What she was trying to get across was how reality was always lensed. And the easiest way to do this was to point to the seventeenth century. There the telescope and the microscope expanded the human imagination at both ends. The great vision of falling bodies which opens *Paradise Lost* would not have been possible without Galileo's telescope. The English poet had visited the Italian scientist. Milton even pays a handsome tribute to him in Book One. Now in fact we don't know how far back in history the invention of the telescope goes. We're not sure what the *merkhet* of the Egyptians was; or the 'queynte mirours' and 'perspectives' mentioned in Chaucer. Roger Bacon's 'glasses or diaphanous bodies' were evidently optical devices, and in the sixteenth century Thomas Digges and John Dee both appear to have made use of 'optic tubes' of some sort, but as far as we know they employed them solely for the magnification of terrestrial objects, to bring faraway visions closer to the eye.

The truly momentous year in the history of this device, the one which had made its use obligatory and shifted the perceptions of humankind irrevocably, redefining in the process the extremities of perception, was 1609 to 1610, when Galileo stared through the telescope he had made for himself. Here Sylvie drew a red line down the side of her margin. She must get this across clearly, or there was no point in any of them being there at all. So what did Galileo see? Lionel, will you take your beady little eyes off my legs for two bloody minutes, and focus on the overhead projection please?

Galileo saw that the Milky Way was more crammed with stars than anyone had previously dreamt, and that Jupiter had four planets, previously undetected. He could see a covering of earthshine on the moon's surface, our own sunny reflection handed back into the darkness of space, but noted also our moon's asperities, its ragged, pock-marked surface, its irregularities and protruberances. Aristotelianiasm began to die there and then, for there was not, as the Greek philosopher had asserted and the European intellectual tradition had maintained for nearly two thousand years, perfection in the celestial sphere. The same laws applied up there as apply down here. This fitted in nicely with Galileo's previous discoveries: that bodies fall, all bodies fall, unless a force acts upon them with sufficient potency to prevent them from so doing. Soon enough everyone would have to accept that the planets didn't move in the celestial perfection of circles either, but described instead a circuit of imperfection, the gravitationally distorted ellipse. Soon everyone in Europe who could afford it, wanted to have one of these telescopes. Galileo tried to make sure he had a few spares with him whenever he performed his demonstrations before princes, since even scientific geniuses need to make a living. And later that year when Galileo's book, *Sidereus Nuncius*, was printed, every fellow of means had to get hold of a copy. Sir Henry Wotton wrote a letter to the Earl of Salisbury on March 13, 1610, in which he said that the work 'is come abroad this very day'. Pirated editions were soon far more numerous than the authorised imprints. The heavens were at last yielding their secrets, though some of the defenders of heaven itself weren't best pleased at this turn of events.

The world had changed, then, and changed for ever – through lenses. The telescope started to habituate the mind to a vast-ness never previously conceived. Then the microscope extended perception in the other direction. Robert Hooke's *Micrographia* had become one of the most famous books in the world soon after its publication in 1665. When Pepys collected his copy, he sat up until two in the morning reading it, and described it as 'the most ingenious book that ever I read in my life.' Lenses alter our perception of reality and the old reality never entirely comes back again.

Now what I want you all to do, Sylvie said to her imaginary

audience, is to consider this week how many of the images in your memories, and how many of the images before your eyes, arrive through lenses. If you think it's less than 50%, then I'd suggest you're not thinking hard enough. Each single one of us is a photographic, microscopic, telescopic and cinematic museum. And we barely notice. We've become our own images. We've become the afterlife of our own images.

Through a Lens Backwards

While Sylvie was delivering this lecture the next day, Owen sat at home and waited for the doorbell to ring. Which it duly did. Johnny Tamworth had come to deliver the advance DVD of *Deva*. Owen had forgotten how well he knew Johnny. This was happening every day now. A void suddenly filled up with a voice, a face, an embrace. The space was there to be filled. Only one clue was required. Owen stared down at the familiar stubble of grey hair, the wire-rimmed glasses, the brackish little beard. Johnny was somehow simultaneously fastidious and tainted. Owen liked him for it.

'It's powerful, Owen, if that makes you feel any better about things. We're still hoping to hold the screening in a couple of months. But there's a big argument going on now about where and when it could be run. I'm half-inclined to cut most of the warehouse scene, to be honest. That's the one causing all the problems. Inevitably.' That was right. They almost always had problems of one sort or another, didn't they? But they got there in the end. Johnny knew his way around. Owen didn't want to think about this particular problem at all. Certainly not the warehouse scene. It was at the end of a very dark corridor, anthracite black, and he was more than happy to leave it there. To leave it all there along with the word Alex.

'Did you bring the camera?'

'Yes. But what is it exactly you want to do, Owen?'

'Will you trust me?'

'I think I sometimes trust you altogether too much.'

'Just film. Don't worry about the soundtrack in the café. It will be a voice-over when we edit. Hand-held. Documentary stuff.'

Twenty minutes later they were in the café, and the same woman with the thick-lensed glasses was staring over at them warily as Johnny pointed his video camera at her. With video, they were mobile and unencumbered with film crews. They could do what they liked.

'It's for a feature about Chester,' Owen said, 'and its more notable characters.' Then more softly, to Johnny: 'Film the table.'

'How do you mean?'

'The surface, the stains, the butt-marks. Give me close-ups of the table. Linger on it as though it were some precious medieval manuscript. That's the way it felt. Like the long water-shot in Tarkovsky's *Stalker*. Let the camera look at everything as though it had never seen it before.'

'I suppose it hasn't, if you think about it.'

Then they went to the hostel. 'Just walk in casually,' Owen said, and as they stepped past the man in his little glass box of an office, he smiled and said, 'Don't worry, Walter, it's all been arranged.'

'Has it?' Johnny asked as they went up the stairs.

'No. But we'll be out of here in no time.'

They walked down the corridor to the room. Alfred was sitting on the bed, as usual, his Bible open on his lap before him.

'You've brought a friend.'

'This is John Tamworth, the film-maker I told you about. We're going to do a bit of filming. You don't mind do you?' He didn't wait for an answer. 'Actually you'll need the sound on for this bit. Pan very slowly between the empty bed and Alfred. Who was it sat there last week, Alfred?' Alfred looked at them both with extreme suspicion before answering slowly.

'A man who had lost his memory. Found himself in the middle of a mystery play. But he was still full of words that had their own memories. So maybe his memories didn't really matter. Maybe his own memories had only really got in the way of the real memories underneath. How am I doing? How's the audition going?' Owen looked at John, suddenly focusing, his lens probing Alfred's face. I think he might be beginning to see the point, Owen thought. Then Alfred turned down to the Bible on his lap and started reading from it.

'And the voice which I heard from heaven spake unto me again and said, "Go and take the little book which is open in the hand of the angel which standeth upon the sea and upon the earth."

'And I went unto the angel, and said unto him, "Give me the little book." And he said unto me, "Take it, and eat it up; and it shall make thy belly bitter, but it shall be in thy mouth sweet as honey." And I took the little book out of the angel's hand, and ate it up; and it was in my mouth sweet as honey: and as soon as I had eaten it, my belly was bitter.'

'Alfred is a great Bible-reader, Johnny. He's read it right through many times.'

Afterwards, Owen insisted they drive to Llandudno. Johnny didn't like this. He'd had had no prior notification. Owen did this to him; took over his life as though there were never any other demands upon him, as though there wasn't anyone else in the world apart from Owen. That, for what it was worth, was his personal theory about Owen's amnesias: they were a way of clearing the world of everyone but himself. Clearing the world of all the debris that wasn't Owen Treadle. But he went, all the same. As usual. Whatever else Owen was, he was rich in suggestiveness. Rich in the potency of his own will. And if his instincts pointed him in a certain direction, it was usually worth going there on a visit, to see what he'd sniffed on the wind.

So they drove to Llandudno.

'Film the sky,' Owen commanded.

'Film the road.'

'Film the estuary over there.'

'Film the hard shoulder.'

Then they were there. On the pier, looking back at the arc of houses along the front. Down on the beach, focusing on the incoming waves. They went to the small hotel. They only wanted the room for an hour. The landlady seemed hostile, particularly when she realised she was being filmed. Johnny was uncomfortable with this, as usual, but Owen had insisted, as usual. 'We walk in filming. I need to see the expression on her face before she has time to decide which expression to put there.'

'Thirty pounds,' Owen said. 'We'll only be an hour. Shan't make any mess. Promise.'

Bed. Dressing table. The mirror. The camera could see the mirror, but the mirror couldn't see the camera, of course, only the room. Then out of the window. The street. The lower reaches of the Orme.

'Long shots, Johnny. Give yourself plenty of time.'

Then they were on their way home.

'How bad is it?' Owen asked as they drove.

'A fucking mess. I wouldn't bother remembering anything if I were you. I'll let you know when it's safe to return to the land of memory.'

'What did I do, Johnny?'

'What you normally do, Owen. Forget the distinctions.'

'Which ones?'

'Between living a life and having it written. Between making an image and being one. Alex, Owen. Alex Gregory. Remember her? You'd better do because memory's all that's left. Apart from the film we put her in: *Deva*.'

A Man of Peace

Owen sat in the small café down by the river and nibbled at a toasted cheese and tomato sandwich. He wondered who had invented toasting. Had it been an accident? A primitive figure sitting too near the fire on a winter evening?

The man came in. He was wearing a hat that had once been white, a seaside hat, an ersatz panama, entirely impractical and out of place, soaked through now from the rain. His glasses had steamed up out there and he let them perch on the end of his dripping nose, where they couldn't have been much use for visibility. He walked to the middle of the floor, bowed three times, removed his hat and began to speak. To everyone and no one.

'I do not look for trouble. My father never looked for it either. He was a man of peace and I am very much his son. I did not invent my troubles; I inherited them. We've all got holes in our head but we don't all have gypsies camping in them. Midnight dances. Flamenco guitars. Rubbish that has to be taken away by the council.'

'Toast, Samuel?'

'Two slices with butter and marmalade.'

'Why don't you sit down and get comfortable, then?' The woman in the white overall behind the counter looked across to Owen and smiled.

'Don't trouble yourself about him, love. He was caught worrying sheep again at the weekend, weren't you Samuel?'

The man had sat down but now stood up once more.

'I do not seek trouble, but it follows me around all the same. Doesn't it, Bethany?'

'You've got cognitive deficits, haven't you love?'

'More of them than you've had hot dinners. And now I am abused on the street.'

'Who's been abusing you out on the street, then?'

'A tall lad with ginger hair.'

'Lot's of freckles? A ring on his nose?'

'That's the one.'

'Nathaniel. Little bugger. Knew his mother. Imogen. She wasn't all she seemed either. Her name was lah-di-dah but nothing else about her was. What did he do this time?'

'He called me an old wanker. Now I do not look for trouble. Like my father I am essentially a man of peace. I know that I am old but I'm not senile, funnily enough. I've always been this way. Just as bonkers when I was twenty.'

'You've got Aspergers, haven't you love? And dyspraxia. And lots and lots of cognitive deficits.'

'Various psychological dysfunctions. A hole in my head like my father before me. And why wanker? I know we live in a surveillance society but there are no CCTV cameras underneath my eiderdown, not that I'm aware of, anyway. What goes on between the sheets . . . I mean my nocturnal activities are my own affair. A man of peace should be left in peace.'

'Don't take any notice of that Nathaniel. He's on his way to becoming . . . ' She faltered.

'An adult male inebriate,' he suggested brightly, which seemed to fit the bill. Bethany nodded.

'Got it in one, so you can't be entirely bonkers, can you? Now sit down and eat your toast. Here it is.' He did as he was told.

'I should be put away, shouldn't I Bethany? But then I

suppose I will be before long. In a pine box. Put away for ever in that.' He looked across at Owen. 'And might I ask your trade, sir?'

Owen found himself at a loss for words. He simply smiled and the old man smiled back.

'You'd be surprised how many people lose the power of speech when I'm around.'

'Only wish you had that effect on bloody Nathaniel out there.'

That evening Owen played the videos and DVDs of his own work, all except one. Each time a new setting came into view, he was there. He wasn't at home; he was there. A night in Zürich, and the club where the female entertainers doubled as hostesses. They had had to keep the camera hidden, though at least one of the girls had cottoned on to what they were doing within half an hour. They had slipped her an extra hundred francs. She made sure the camera saw plenty of thigh. Then the Corbusier House, and its orientally low tables. Swiss mountains as the train ran along beneath them, then the suddenness of the grid of streets in New York, Manhattan reaching for the skies. The traffic's entrance to Tokyo, as though the camera were entering a vast concrete car-park. Punts along the Cam, a weedy, willowy, watery progress to nowhere in particular. Dark skies over northern cities, millstone grit houses in despairing rows. Children with large Indian eyes, beseeching the weather to go away for ever. Batting and bowling with an upturned milk-crate for a wicket.

A scene off the western coast of Ireland. He remembered filming that, he could even feel the boat still lurching beneath him. Johnny had kept them out there for six hours, for he could be demanding too: he knew precisely what he wanted. And what he wanted here was the right light. The camera assistant had retched three times over the side, and the Irish skipper had remained grimly smiling, barely saying a word to anyone. Johnny wanted the light for that sequence to be right, and wouldn't consider turning back to harbour until they had it on film. Wharfedale at dawn, looking as though the mist might wreathe itself into a ghost. Finally he couldn't take any more. Owen felt as though an orgy of images had been rioting inside him. He'd kept putting one film in after another, fast-forwarding, halting, taking out the tape, then trying a different one. He had no idea where Sylvie was. At midnight he finally phoned the Institute. Answering machine.

'It's Owen. Hope you're well. I'm going for a drive.'

He drove in the dark to Snowdonia. Edged his way up a starvecrow road. Stopped on a hilltop. Stared up at the sky to see the plough. It occurred to him that you would be able to see that at the same moment from a bothie on the west coast of Scotland, wouldn't you? Right now. You'd see the very same thing. If you were a young woman with a ruined psyche. Starving to death as a matter of conviction.

At that precise moment, Henry Allardyce was dreaming. It was a terrible dream, but he had dreamt it so many times before that he almost knew his way through it. He already knew that this was a horror that would end. Florence was flooded as it had been four decades before. The Arno had set about drowning what was left of the Renaissance. Men waded in to their waists to heave out gilded pictures, as though seizing vast, glittering fish, subaquean treasures of silver and gold. The Arno merged with the Shropshire Severn in his dream, and his Picassos were sinking in the water. Henry was thrashing about, trying to get hold of the pictures, but they were drifting away from him. The vast creatures bellowed as they drowned. My minotaurs, Henry thought. No one ever taught them how to swim.

At the same time in Liverpool Sylvie was imagining the eye of a ghost, its lens a filament no thicker than gossamer, separating two kingdoms. That would have been what he'd be looking through then, if the ghost of John Lennon had come up the Mersey that night, a stow-away on a transatlantic liner, the stately progress like the bleb of a glacier, snouting its way in to the Albert Dock and then creeping up past Paradise Road and along to Rodney Street, swooping in through the window, one of those bats in Bram Stoker's *Dracula*, but making no noise, a quieter spirit now, there being no wars or shouting on the other side; only to discover Sylvie Ashton at her table in the Signum staring at his picture on her wall, and then resuming his domicile inside his photograph once more, that being where most ghosts take up residence sooner or later. There was something about Lennon's features and voice, the combination of the domineering, even bullying, look and manner, and the ceaseless vulnerability, that continually made Sylvie ponder things. Minotaur. The bellow in the cavern and then later the whimper as the steel shoots in. One life: a labyrinth.

She let Owen's message go on the answering machine, then crept over the corridor to listen at Hamish's door. Tap tap tap, sure enough. You could hear him snaring all incoming calls. Snooping little bastard.

'Good-night Hamish,' she called out gently. 'Sleep well.' Then *sotto voce*: 'You kilted wanker.'

Hamish's head was round his door before she could make it back.

'What? What did you just say?'

'I said good-night, Hamish. Sleep well. God's watching over you tonight, so thank Her.'

She lay in the dark and listened for the boats, as the ghost of John Lennon listened along with her up on her wall. So was she leaving Owen then, was she, finally up and off? Until his latest erasure she had been pretty convinced he had already left her. She had only been waiting for the announcement. Then instead there was . . . all that. Alex. *Deva*. It struck her as curious: what an intermittent requirement sex could be. For her anyway. There had been a time at the beginning with Owen when it had been incessant. Come to think of it, Owen had continued pretty incessantly, but not always with her. Now what did Henry want? Henry wanted to be comforted, she reckoned. With red wine and warm embraces. That particular minotaur wanted his half-sister Ariadne to take out her famous bobbin, thread herself through the complications of his life to the centre of the riddle, and hold him tightly in the night while he moaned. Moaned and thrashed. He didn't want his bed to be a grave he shared with his dead wife. He wanted a resurrection girl in there to bring his darkness back to life. But she couldn't. She liked Henry but she didn't love him, and she wasn't old enough or desperate enough for money to pretend there was no difference any more. There was a difference. She had loved a husband once and the loving had exhausted her; but she was still not prepared to pretend there was no difference. But she couldn't afford to live in the house in Chester alone. Was that why she had started sleeping over here in Liverpool so often, trying out the alternatives? Seeing what life might be like without her lovely house? So what was to be done then? Buggered if she knew. Better get some sleep anyway. Tom Helsey was lecturing in the morning for her *Afterlife of Images* course, and she was slated to introduce him.

In the morning she emerged from the bathroom, having showered and put on her make-up. As she opened the door she saw Hamish in his dressing-gown, a towel over his arm, a look of practised impatience on his face.

'Morning Hamish.'

'If you are planning on staying over often, we'd better come to an understanding about washing arrangements and suchlike in the morning.'

'We need more facilities, Hamish. An Institute of such distinction needs more than one bathroom, surely. I think you should have one entirely to yourself.'

The Burn Lecture

She was trying to explore different ways of imaging the world, different ways of lensing it, in the process abolishing distance, and as usual cancelling time, so she had invited Tom over from Physics. She'd heard he gave lively lectures. Never heard any herself. She introduced him. He walked up to the podium smiling and switched on the overhead projector. A flaring image was illuminated on the screen. He started speaking.

'Once the collapse begins, then you know the real brightness must get started. A brightness compared to which every other lamp in your life was nothing but marshlight through drizzle. Now you will be needing those powers of ten you always thought were useless, only employed by scientists like me. Have a good look at this image. It'll scorch your sockets with zeroes. A supernova, even in its humdrum pre-celebrity status as mere star, was always a power to be reckoned with. Gravity might be the weakest of the four forces we believe control the universe, but it's still strong enough, believe me. Don't, whatever you do, underestimate it on your way home tonight. It's what brings us back to earth each time after our little excursions.

'Your subject, Sylvie has told me, is how we make images of the reality we find around us; how we contain inside the mind realities which are a billion times larger than the brain. We have to reduce the universe one thousand million million million million times to fit it inside our skulls. That's a serious compression of the image. And then the image itself lives on and starts to change us.

'Once more we're back with that theme we never seem to escape for long: the biographical imperative. If you lived entirely inside a blue shade, then every reality you saw would be blue. And there would be no blue, since blue would simply be reality. Well we live inside biography, and so we assign births and deaths and careers to everything we encounter. From the carrot to the elephant; from a tiny satellite to the universe itself. And so we talk of "the life of stars", playing Boswell to the Great Cham of nature. We might even occasionally catch their births – a little dribble of light in the Orion Nebula signifying a beginning. One of the minor cosmic creatures announcing its nativity, mewling and puking in the nurse's arms. Our own star, source of all life and warmth, the dear Sun we've so often worshipped as God, is already in mid-career. The protons burn efficiently to helium, the material is consumed, the energy released. And so it goes on, most usefully for our present purposes, but not for ever of course. Each nucleic metamorphosis announces our mortality. If not quite yet, you'll be pleased to hear. We turn everything into biographies, we tell each other stories all the time, because we must die.

'But now imagine a star vastly more massive than our sun. It is burning, finding a tighter form of organization for itself, which is what all burning is. The difference between the looser and the tighter form, the trimmer atomic organization of its destination, is released as energy. Part of this energy turns into photons. Light. And from such concentrations of light in the night sky we constructed our first calendars; even fathomed our fates, pondered who and what we were. And where we were, how the years roll round us. No photons, no images.

'The gravitational force, a force too vast for anything but

mathematics and poetry to approach, pulls in with relentless insistence. But the nuclear heart of the matter has a big enough reply as long as enough fuel is being pumped into its blazing furnace by the nano-second. Then at one moment, arriving at one infinitesimal iota of a dot in this gargantuan chronicle, the balance falters, by the smallest particle and for the briefest measure of time. That's all it takes. And as with us so with the planets too: life can go on for as long as it likes, but death only has its one good moment and so tends to make the best of it. There's a rage against the dying of the light. In a few milliseconds, gravity suddenly has more resources than the burn that's been for so many ages resisting it.

'The matter implodes, an object ten times the size of the Sun crashes towards its own nucleus. The force of its motion is so astounding that even the equations blink – the laws of nature seem to go briefly into reverse, though they haven't, of course. The mass impacts beyond its natural point of equilibrium, in and in it goes with such relentless momentum, such a vast elastic nightmare of distortion like a bowstring pulled in every direction at once until it hits the distended fulcrum-point and fires out a galaxy of light. WHOOSH. Enough light to annihilate all the darkness you've ever seen, or ever will.

'We're a long way off, don't forget that – a mathematical distance, which means so far away that not even a genius could truly imagine it. The rest of us simply keep on writing out the numbers. You'll need a lot of zeroes. Don't ever confuse calculation with imagining; we're touching the extremities here. But even so, even though we're so far away that we don't know whether to measure this distance in time or kilometres, and instead muddle through with a mixture of the two, confusing almost everyone in the process with our talk of light years, even so, at this moment, the human world catches its breath: old men with grubby beards climb out of bed and stare through the window in silence. They make a gift of the energy in their bare feet to the floorboards, and don't even notice. Tears fill their rheumy old eyes. They know that a new sort of king is to be born in the east. They stare at the sleeping face on the pillow and remember all the hope they once saw there. At least they have lived to see the longed-for portent. So now they can die with bright eyes.

'Nova was the word Galileo used. *Nova stella*, a new star. He saw one in 1604. A novel light off there in the firmament, to be riddled and equated and named. But we have made distinctions he'd never even dreamt of, so we have added *super-nova*. Which isn't a new star at all, of course, but a dying one. The manifestation in the visible spectrum of an apocalyptic terminus. Something so vast its distance is an integral part of its perception, and we arrive along with the belated shower of light to write its obituary. The life of stars, you see. Your life in the stars. And it's true: the horoscopists have a point after all. We are made out of material which a celestial body provided, cooked in the fire of its mighty collapse. We're all of us stars really. We've all blazed with light up there in our time. It wasn't only Elvis shining in his sequin suit as we bent our necks to catch him. We've all been brilliant up there once, however dull we've become in the interim down here since.

'This one in the picture they call 1987A. It fair takes your breath away, doesn't it, the mystical soul of the modern astronomer. Confronted by one of the most imponderable events ever perceived by humankind, the unmistakable flash and blaze of fate in the heavens, our contemporary mental cosmonaut reaches deep into his innermost region and announces this rubric to his litany: *1987A*. Remark the lyricism that engulfs him when he finally encounters wonder. 1 . . . 9 . . . 8 . . . 7. And A of course. Don't forget alpha, the birth-letter to which our supernova constitutes an omega. *1987A*. Maybe it sounds better chanted in Aramaic. Who knows, it might describe an occult harmony, a Pythagorean cave hidden deep in the psyche. Or it might be simply another postscript to the *Anglo-Saxon Chronicle*.'

He stopped there and looked out carefully as though trying to fathom whether or not their eyes might have started to glaze. How many little dead stars off there in the lecture hall, as the scientist plays Copernicus to the elliptical orbits of their attention? These our revels now are ended, Sylvie thought. Time to switch off the projector, Tom. Time for coffee. Time to leave the universe. Or was it to rejoin it?

'It was excellent,' she said as she poured him his coffee. 'No photons, no images. The miniaturisation of reality.'

'They often take their time arriving. I'm interested in your work, what I've heard of it. How about a drink some time?'

'Fine. Check your diary and give me a ring.' She tried to remember whether or not he was married. There'd been that bit about the head on the pillow that had once filled you with hope. He was tall and blond and attractive, though perhaps a little too aware of the fact. He liked to put it about a bit, didn't he? Alison had told her about him. Said he wasn't to be trusted; there'd been some trouble with a student. Might make a change from tall dark Owen, all the same, or small greying Henry, wouldn't it? We're only talking about a drink, for God's sake. Still, you'd better decide what you're going to do in life, girl, or you might find you're already doing it before any decision gets made. And what would Daddy have had to say about that?

Water Goddess

Henry Allardyce stood in his garden and stared at the river. They said the new defences would prevent flooding, but he wasn't entirely convinced. Any signs of the water-level rising started that old dark sensation inside, a murky vortex of turbulence. He could still smell the filth from last time: the world's sump emptied on your floor. Water rising up towards the minotaur's tail.

The bell rang and Martin Frome walked in, clutching for once not a national but a local paper.

'Just over the river there.' He pointed with his copy of the newspaper. 'An Indian family bought an Alsatian.'

'I thought Indians didn't like dogs.'

'That's what surprised everyone. There's always a sign over their shops isn't there? No dogs allowed, unless you're blind. Everyone reckoned they thought dogs were unclean and dangerous. Turns out in this case, everyone was right.' It transpired that it was in fact precisely the uncleanly menace of the creature that had attracted Mr Patel to the purchase. He was afraid of burglars, rapists, racist thugs in balaclavas who might break in to his house in the night. His fear was perhaps exaggerated round these parts, but not if you took account of where he'd been living a little while before. Such things had happened in the northern town he'd chosen as his previous address, if not exactly frequently, then with enough frequency to merit his anxiety.

'Anyway, he bought the dog. The dog had never been given a name, it was simply called "Dog", and since this was the same word that was used in their native Urdu to refer to untouchable and filthy humans, its resonance endeared no one in the family to the animal. He kept it in the garden. It had a makeshift kennel where it usually defecated. It was chained. It was never taken in to the house, never touched or stroked. Mr Patel worked out precisely what the minimum food for a dog of that breed and size should be, and then gave it a little less. This was on the advice of a friend of his at work who'd informed him that the best guard dogs were always kept undernourished. This made them muscled-up and hostile, very light sleepers. Usually it was fed curry, which probably left its digestive system raw and angry anyway.

'Just before midnight he'd go out and poke the dog in the belly with a stick. This provoked it to a fury which it was never far from the edge of anyway, and it would immediately start barking for up to an hour.' A feral, grimacing, hungry bark, the neighbours had reported; a noise of hunting savagery that would surely deter any young thugs, even those whose heads were raddled with drugs, from venturing near his garden, his house, or his children. Martin now started reading the rest of the account from the newspaper article.

All of the members of Mr Patel's well-dressed, well-fed, very polite family looked upon the dog as a necessary evil. They wished that it didn't have to bark so much and wake them, but they accepted with a mild resentment that this was the price of their security. All of them accepted this, except for the youngest of all, little Serena, whose lexicon was still very much her own affair. For her the word dog didn't signify humans whom you must not bed or marry or even break bread with, but simply one more curious creature in the curious menagerie of the world. The dog, its bared teeth, its jangling chain, its ceaseless hunger, and the derangement it was now beginning to suffer from lack of physical contact with any other creatures, human or canine, none of this signified anything whatsoever to the little girl. Which was why, when the back door was inadvertently left open late one afternoon, she tottered out and kept walking on her stout little legs until she came within the chain's growling circle.

Martin held the paper before Henry and Henry looked at the photograph. She'd needed eighty-seven stitches to sew her head back up and stop it from leaking blood the way a smashed tomato in the road bleeds juices. There was still a query hovering over her survival. The dog without a name had already been destroyed. Mr Patel was in the process of being charged with wanton cruelty to a domestic animal, and there was now no more barking in the night along the avenue. Henry continued to stare at the photograph in silence, long after Martin had gone, leaving the paper with him.

Henry sometimes wondered if there might have been a change of lighting – in the world, he meant, not in his gallery. In there the lighting was exactly the same as it has been the day he moved in: a little dim unless the sun shone through one of the crooked windows. But he thought it might have grown fractionally darker outside. He only caught fragments of the news, but it seemed that people over the world had taken to mass slaughter with a fresh enthusiasm. We were all off again, it seemed. Fate's appetite for flesh was as strong as ever.

He went and sat in the Picasso Room. The eyes of the minotaur were on him. They were all hungry, that was for sure, but for what? What would their food be this time?

The Memory Book

He ordered a pint and sat down next to two middle-aged men, sitting before their drinks with that curious British demeanour of stoicism in the face of the task that lies ahead. Half of the pint gone; only another half to go. We can get there. As Owen was opening the book, the man nearest to him spoke.

'You remember those signs that used to say *PLEASE TAKE YOUR RUBBISH HOME WITH YOU*?'

'Mmm.'

'My daughter appears to have taken that rather literally. Which is why I'm about to acquire a primitive hunter-gatherer for a son-in-law. Encountered on a caravan site, I believe.'

'What does he do?'

'Drugs.'

Owen was already turning back the pages of the book inside himself. He was aware that there was a sensation growing. It wasn't a memory, not yet, because it wasn't fully focused yet. It might have been a memory once; it would be again. Before very long, he suspected. At the moment it was a region of darkness, growing in intensity. Does darkness have intensity, or is that only light? He couldn't remember. Have to ask Johnny. Johnny knew all about optics. He kept turning the pages, as though looking for a title. There seemed to be many illustrations of the different shapes memory had travelled under: Plato's wax tablet, a house with different rooms, each one filled with its own accoutrements, palaces, abbeys,

cathedrals, a computer, a holograph, a palimpsest, an archae-
ological dig, Freud's magical writing pad, and, over and over
again, a labyrinth. Was there a minotaur sitting at the heart of
this fucking labyrinth then, or only Henry Allardyce with a
glass of red wine? He closed the book and sat staring at the bar.
Something was about to arrive and he knew it.

*

Sylvie put the video Ali had given her into its machine. A young
girl was walking up and down, or trying to. Her legs were bent out
of shape, and her gait was a constant battle not to fall over. As she
struggled a voice-over began.

*You have 100,000 goes at it before you get it right. Then your mind
stores that particular manoeuvre – left leg up as right leg goes down
again – and you stop falling over. That's fine. You're only twelve
months old. You have all the time in the world and energy to burn.*

*But what if you're not twelve months, but twelve years old, and your
legs still don't work right? They never have. You never walk farther
than a hundred metres. You go to school in a wheelchair. And you
don't have energy to burn because you're already burning up far too
much of it to force your body through the irregular movements that
constitute your abnormal gait? What then?*

Still the little girl struggled up and down, this way then that.

*This little girl's bipedal locomotion is so poor that she never walks
far. We view her on a video. What can we do? The girl has splints, but
she doesn't like wearing them. In the trade we call this 'non-
compliance'; it's far from uncommon. The splints are large, and hardly
fashionable. Physiotherapy? We're doing that, but it won't make much
difference. Surgery is possible, but the parents are unenthusiastic.
Results are not guaranteed and the scarring would be permanent.*

*What is our narrative of expectation? That's all about the
expenditure of energy, which in a precise sense is the 'cost' of this
disability. It is surely an oddity of human history how often we come to*

understand ourselves as a result of studying our own creations. These days we negotiate neuroscience by comparing the functioning of a computer with that of a brain. In the nineteenth century we studied the steam engines we had built, so as to maximise their efficiency. What did any system do with the energy put into it? It converted some into work, the rest it lost. Whenever a steam engine transmitted heat to its surroundings it was losing energy, which in a machine of perfect efficiency it would have turned into work instead. Such studies led to the formulation of the laws of thermodynamics. And we can look at the body as a system of energy conversion in the same way. Statistics tell us the approximate amount of energy you should be expending by walking. If your legs have been buckled since infancy then this amount will show as much higher than normal. Everything costs too much. Daily life is simply too expensive. And it will get more expensive the older the girl gets.

And then there was no more voice-over, only the film of the little girl making her painful and ungainly way up and down the lab, this way and that, with legs buckled too far out of shape for their purpose. The persistence of vision, the afterlife of images. Sylvie watched it in silence.

Euland

As Sylvie began the long incline that pointed down towards the Birkenhead Tunnel, she was listening to that tape of Paul Darcy which her student had lent her. The song, in a minor key, achieved some curious effects by combining unexpected instruments. There was an acoustic guitar, an oud, a soprano sax:

> *There's been an earthquake in the Philippines, a flashflood*
> >   *in NYC*
> *Everybody's searching high and low, no one notices me*
> *Headlights hit the windows, nervous drinkers hit the floor*
> *Sirens are wailing, please tell me who they're wailing for*
> *The labyrinth's alive tonight as silence is transformed into heat*
> *I heard somebody shout they're turning mystery to meat*
> *I can hear the angry wind pounding and pounding on the door*
> *Blindfolds and chains, and the traffic's ever-growing roar*

He'd obviously been reading some of her books, looking at some of her pictures. Maybe he'd been having an affair with Henry too. There was no copyright on this material. The student had also given her a book about him. It appeared to have been written by a once-faithful roadie, pimp and all-round servicer of Darcy's requirements.

The writer tried to remember at one point how many women he must have put Darcy's way. Going down to the auditorium during the interval to pick up the chosen creatures and get them back-stage passes with a minimum of fuss. To let them in to the light behind the darkness; or was it the dark behind the light? For at least one three-month period, pander and lord were both only too aware that each one of these chosen creatures was being infected with a non-specific, but undoubtedly anti-social, virus. Not that this stopped Darcy going at it like a rat up a drainpipe. As his Boswell now put it: 'Paul Darcy is an unscrupulous fucker, but on a good night, he's still one of the best singers in the world.' And in between getting pissed, getting stoned, and getting laid, he obviously read a lot. Everybody's in this bloody labyrinth these days, she thought, and made a mental note to phone Henry later.

Sylvie spent the first few hours of the day in the Signum's library. This was the heart of the building, and the real reason it existed at all. Friedrich Euland, a refugee from Vienna in the 1930s, had chosen to risk the bombs falling on his precious book collection in Liverpool rather than have them fall on his precious book collection in London. He had come to detest all crowds and Liverpool was smaller; it was as simple as that. His British devotee, James Almond, who subsequently wrote his intellectual biography, *Euland: Melancholy Anatomist*, doubted that Euland had gone out much by that stage in any case, his psychological condition being so severe that the only place he could feel comfortable was surrounded by his books and prints. No air-raid warnings would ever have evacuated him. Almond argued, with some conviction, that Euland's disablement for normal life facilitated his thought. He drew parallels with Darwin and Proust. Sylvie was sitting under the alabaster bust. Euland was a small man, with a large moustache, his gaze fixed perennially elsewhere; anywhere, it seemed, but here.

He had gathered together a rewarding collection of scientific images from over the centuries. She had picked up some of her obsessions from him, though he would surely have been astounded at the destinations she was now carrying them towards. We constellate reality, form images of it, challenge it, destroy it, form new images, but certain motifs seem to remain constant. The question was this: when technology transformed the possibilities of image-making, did this alter our underlying psychology, or merely amplify it? Had the pictures from the Hubble Telescope changed our sense of being in the world, or merely extended it by powers of ten? Once only the monarch was the centre of the circle of the world, his or her face impressed on every coin. Then technology had permitted all sorts of new images, a proliferation of them beyond any anticipation, and what had we done with those images? Had we displaced the notion that anyone was the centre of the circle of the world, or merely multiplied it? The astonishing fecundity of the images of musical celebrities, even their voices at the centre of those circles of the world that were once black vinyl and now shiny metal, playing from millions of machines all over the world, little gleaming tabernacles, this fecundity of voice-imprinting and image-making hadn't necessarily shifted the basic psychic parameters at all. She suspected that this was what Euland had come to believe by the end, and she believed it too. What did we call them, as they shone up there, and we crooked our necks? Stars. What did we call Elvis? The king. How brightly they had shone, and how everyone had bent the knee, offered the body, paid the coin. We were still in a glittering kingdom, living with the afterlife of images.

Euland had no doubt that worship, often of the most murderous variety, was an ineradicable part of the human mind. But what had we left ourselves to worship, in the vast clearings of modernity? The world of commodities, according to Euland, expressed itself philosophically not in the works of Marx and Engels, but in the words of nihilism. Unattributable makings issuing from the engine of manufacture, an engine without purpose except to enlarge its own productiveness. This machine of creation made commodities the way, in Darwin's scheme, the blind idiot called Nature made creatures – some for life, others for destruction, with no moral filament to distinguish between them, except their 'fitness for survival', a phrase Euland could never encounter without horror, because it made him fear that Nazism was not a hideous deformation, but an emanation from the brute core of human existence itself.

He had become greatly preoccupied after the war with the figure of Magda Goebbels. He felt that she had stepped out of Euripides and into the history of Europe: Medea slaughtering her children, not because she was in a rage at Jason any more, but simply at the thought of a world without Hitler, a de-Nazified world unfit to inherit her little ones. So she poisoned her beloved chicks and then allowed herself to be put to death in turn. She had once, noted Euland, been thought the most famous mother in Germany. Beautiful children spawned by her malignant dwarf of a husband.

The book before her was Euland's *Notebooks and Papers*. Sylvie often returned to them, and then extrapolated at a rate that had begun to alarm even her. What she was trying to do now was link images and mirrors. The technological link was simple: *speculum* and speculation, mirrors in telescopes and miscroscopes, facilitating images and the de-coding of images, mirrors in cameras doing the same. She was less convinced that the psychological aspect had been properly broached.

For years in the 1960s every time a young man looked in the mirror he wanted to be one of those four faces; the four faces of the Beatles. Or maybe the Stones. Or Dylan. And every time a girl looked into a mirror she wanted to have one of those same faces looking back at her. And yet John Lennon had to spend the rest of his life trying to find a man there, a human being, no more, no less. A man whose father had walked out on him, and whose mother had been killed by a speeding police car. He knew that the image, whatever its proliferation in millions upon millions of copies, could never replace the face in the mirror. You finally had to come back in solitude to that. The persistence of that vision was irreversible. 'I'm just an ordinary man,' the Beatle cried, to universal incredulity. And yet in one sense of course, he was, for what else could he be? And what did Bob Dylan see when he looked in the mirror? Did he see Robert Zimmerman of Hibbing, Minnesota? Or something entirely different? Did he really see the myth he'd made of himself? Did the same creature come out of the labyrinth as had once gone in?

When the Christian looks at the figure on the cross he sees lots of suffering behind and plenty more on its way. Inescapable anguish and suffering. So offer it all up to God. But what did William Blake see? Glory. Resplendent glory. That's what he said, and there seems no reason to disbelieve him. And what did the Easter Islanders see when they stared up at those vast stony gods they themselves had hewn to palliate the powers that would destroy them anyway? They saw the vast nails that held earth to heaven, and would never come loose. The whole of the island was a mirror to the skies. Were all images mirrors then, to some extent? Did they all simply reflect our beliefs, our wishes and our pain?

Euland saw with great vividness that the ancient categories of rhetoric, the facility to blind and deafen the moral faculties with persuasive power, hadn't been in any way negated or even diluted by modern technologies of communication; they had simply grown greater and greater. He found due cause for terror here. He knew the voices of Hitler and Goebbels, the husband this time not the wife; they had been planted in his head by the radio, but no radio signals could ever take them out again. He had meditated long and hard on the lethal temptation of all verbal magic harnessed to power: a fake enchantment for a disenchanted world, a simplification of reality resulting in murder. A new mirror from which you would emerge transformed, an image replicated over and over again, shaping a new reality, a new kingdom, a new Reich. And you would be one of many. Your identity could be reflected in everyone else's. A consonance of images, since all dissonant ones would have been eradicated. There was one thing of which he had no doubt: in the iconography of power, the sacrifice of any member of the ruling group was always the brief preface to a much greater sacrifice of those outside it.

The facilitating void of the mirror, Sylvie wrote in her note-book, quicksilvered to give you back what you gave it; but not precisely. Left and right stayed the same as they did on the other side of the looking-glass. Only selected elements of reality were reversed. She remembered how Judy Garland sang to the photograph of Clarke Gable in the film. And he was just as real as if he'd been there. Was she meant to be seeing him, or the image of her own desire in which he was reflected?

She wrote down two words at the bottom of the page, followed by a query: Imago . . . phantasmagoria? Then she read the passage from Euland's famous essay, in Almond's translation.

No escape from images in language. Words carry their own history inside them, like the flesh beneath a turtle's carapace. Etymology: screams and sighs inside that word. Love, hatred, conquest, defeat, birth, death. Some of these words still have fragments of skin attached; some have barely ceased whimpering. Some are locked in the scriptorium, others in the lazar-house. Words are sometimes angels chanting hallelluias, sometimes the befouling of the spirit at the inquisitor's bleak bidding. Mirrors, and so, like mirrors in the houses of the dead, we drape their flashing surfaces with dark sheets. Lock them away in the high room where we keep the dictionaries, those chronicles of suspicion and depravity. Definitions, incantations, monstrous anathemas.

Ariadne's Bobbin

Facilitating Void upon the wall/ Who is the fairest of them all? No answer came the stern reply. You don't get the same class of mirror you did in Snow White's day, that's for sure. Sylvie stared at the flashing light on the telephone. 'Maybe I should just pop over to Hamish and ask him who called.' She pressed the play-back button. Henry.

'There's going to be a pizza here with your name on it tonight, and a nice glass of chianti. Any chance?'

Yes, in fact there was a chance. It was clear-out time in Sylvie's life, and she'd decided she'd better get on with it. Owen's behaviour had finally forced her to a decision, and she now felt it was time to be ruthless all round. She really couldn't afford to drift. She had slid into Henry's arms, more to comfort him than herself. Or had she? That's what she now told herself, anyway. She would tell him tonight that their relationship couldn't go any further. And while she was at it, she would take her notebook and make any final jottings she needed on the Picasso engravings. Her relationship with Owen was finished; any sexual stuff with Henry would be over as of tomorrow morning, though she'd give him one good valedictory night; he'd certainly get his pizza's worth. She'd be his comfort woman and there'd be no hard feelings. The thing she must get on and really finish was her book. It was time to move away from the Signum Institute. What a lot of moving on I'm doing, she thought. She and Henry must stay friends, if it were at all possible, but she had a feeling that Henry was going to need to fill a hole in his life, and that hole might well be filled by someone who wasn't all that keen on seeing Sylvie turning up for her take-away pizza once a month. A fragrant Shrewsbury lady needing permanent company would soon see Sylvie off.

She sat down at the desk and wrote this:

Sylvie's Little Litany

Therianthrope

Minotaur

Picasso

(Henry?)

Persistent Vision
(Abolished in amnesia?)

Owen

Dogs after the inundation – a world without signs

Deva

A water-nymph turned slimy and riverlike

Alex Gregory
(who should have drowned, surely)

Time's widow

Owen

Owen

Bloody fucking Owen. Do it now then.

She picked up the phone and dialled. Owen answered.
'I was wondering if you might make arrangements to go

and stay somewhere else for a while?' He seemed remarkably composed when he spoke.

'You want a divorce, don't you?' She hesitated.

'Yes, I think I do. Stay with a friend, Owen. Just for a while. Would Johnny let you stay with him? I don't want to have to worry about you. Think I might have done enough of that for one lifetime, to be fair.'

Then she phoned Henry.

'I'll come over tonight. Yes, love to. We'll need to have a bit of a chat, I think . . . .Well, quite a serious one, yes.'

As she sat and stared at the picture of the Beatles standing on the dock in Liverpool waiting for the future to arrive, the phone rang again. It was Tom Helsey.

'How about that drink?'

'All right. When?'

'Tomorrow night?'

'Where?'

'The Phil at eight o'clock.'

'See you there.'

*

'So aren't you actually selling any of this stuff then, Henry?'

'Not unless I absolutely have to, no, not the stuff in here. I suppose the day might come.'

'No contradiction between you being a gallery owner, and sitting on all these works you won't let anybody else near?'

'I let you near. You're anybody else. You're here in the Picasso Room. Is that pizza all right?'

'Tastes exactly like the other one.'

'I've noticed that too. They all taste exactly the same. I am, to all intents and purposes, a vegetarian. Technicolour straw seems to be produced to a modular design. The different titles are only meant to distract you.'

'Do many dealers buy work they never mean to sell?'

'Well, one of Picasso's most important early dealers, Uhde, always made a distinction between his collection and his stock. The stock was for sale, the collection wasn't. Having a German name, come 1914 everything he owned was taken by the French state. Amongst the possessions sequestered that day were fifteen Picassos, some of them masterpieces. He'd never tried to sell a single one. I think I'm with Uhde on this. If you love them so much why pass them on? Keep them; give your eyes and soul a treat. Why should I have those astonishing images translated back into rows of figures in a bank? Does that make for civilisation, as you understand it?'

'No. I'm not entirely sure this pizza does either.'

'In Italy, there'd be riots on the street. The rivers would break their banks.'

Henry, as usual, kept offering her more wine, and for once she took it. Her gaze softened and she remembered how much she liked Henry; how gentle he had always been, even in his importunity. She smiled; he smiled back, and poured more chianti into her glass. She was sitting underneath the *Satyr and Sleeping Woman*. There was little enough difference between this satyr and the minotaur, except that his face was a little less bullish. He had uncovered the woman and looked at her with a look of delight and anticipation. He would have her, she thought. He deserved her. And he obviously adored her. This moment, given the tranquillity of their mood, seemed a good one to broach the matter.

'Henry, we need to talk about things.'

'Whichever way you wanted to do it,' he said. 'I don't mind.' She was a little confused by this; it also struck her that she was a little drunk.

'Do what?'

'You know how I feel about you. You've already told me that

you want the relationship with Owen to end, and that would mean you couldn't keep the house in Chester. I'd be happy to come to any arrangement you like. You are welcome to come and stay here on any terms, at any time.'

'I don't love you, Henry.'

'But you like me. I married love twice and found grief both times. Then the last time I married grief, and found love. But she died. She was already dying. Eleanor once said to me that she'd always been dying. I think she was born dying.'

'I can't, Henry.' Something had suddenly brought her close to tears again, but she really couldn't cry at his place twice in a row. She had not anticipated this. Henry had always seemed so stoical and humorous. She didn't want him humiliating himself. She wished she hadn't drunk so much wine. The words forming on her tongue felt recalcitrant.

'Owen and I are . . . getting divorced. I'll have to sell the house in Chester because I won't have enough money coming in to keep it going by myself. But . . . I don't love you enough to live with you, Henry. I'm not sure I can live with anyone else just now. Shall we go to bed?'

Henry was staring at another of the etchings. The minotaur had the woman on his lap, while others looked on, glass in hand. It seemed to take a very long time before he finally answered.

'I think it might be better if we didn't,' he said and smiled. What a sorry smile. 'It would just make matters worse. I'm not keen on valedictory sex. I can't get you out of my mind, Sylvie.'

And that was how Sylvie ended up staying in the other room, being too drunk by that stage to drive back to Chester, or anywhere else. In the morning she crept out to her car, and never spoke to Henry.

She arrived in Chester feeling awful, and wanted only to

change and drive over to Liverpool, where she was teaching in two hours. She dreaded the prospect of seeing Owen. She didn't have to worry. He had already packed some things and gone. *Staying with Johnny*, the note said. Because Sylvie seldom drank too much, she was seldom hung-over. That made the experience all the worse. All she wanted to do was get through her lectures and return home. A house to herself for once. She was gathering up her things before clearing off when the phone rang. Owen? Henry? She thought she'd better answer.

'Hi, it's Tom. Just making sure we're still on for tonight.' She sat back on her chair.

'Well Tom, I'm a bit out of it, actually.'

'So am I. We'll make a great couple. You can tell me your problems; I'll tell you mine.' And before she could think of another thing to say, he'd hung up.

As she walked from the house to the car she saw Jack Jameson, or Gizmo Gus, as she and Owen always called him. He was, as usual, plugged in. A mobile phone was pressed to his ear, as he walked along. He was now the British represent-ative for an American company called Anderton Supplies.

What it appeared to supply was whatever the US Army needed after its latest intervention/invasion/liberation/occup-ation. Satellite phones, paper cups, dried food, medical pro-vision, combat clothing, shades, cigarettes, booze, fuel. The great advantage of all this, from Anderton's point of view, as Jack had pointed out to them one evening, was that it had to manufacture nothing. Who on earth wanted to get involved in manufacturing in this day and age? So, no deleterious design or technology to fret about. All the company needed to do was cherry-pick market winners (or sometimes market-losers, if they were cheap and disposable enough) and then supply them at a premium vast enough to keep its shareholders and directors sweet. The share-price had risen from $1.99 in 1997 to \$30.55 by the end of 2003. Periods of belligerence were good for Anderton's profile. The Iraqi War undoubtedly helped. For every US soldier who fell in combat, Anderton's index register jumped another few cents. Even the dead need body bags, and someone has to supply them, along with all the pharmaceuticals for the wounded. And commanding officers, needing to communicate with the families of the deceased, needed stationery. So whoever else could lose, Anderton couldn't. Sylvie made sure she didn't catch his eye.

That evening Sylvie's student Lionel went to the Phil. Prior to this he had spent several hours trying to make himself attractive to women. After showering and rubbing and squirting and talcing, he had then applied a copious amount of Brilliant Gel to his dark curly hair. Brilliant Gel advertised a 'wet look' that could last for twelve hours. This was good, not because Lionel's hair would otherwise dry out; *au contraire*, as he had recently learnt to say, and very much liked saying. The problem was that Lionel's scalp sweated. Only on social occasions. He could happily toil away at a manual task for hours, and not a drip. But the minute he was in a pub, or on a dance-floor, surrounded by pheromones and perfumes, the scalp would begin to itch and then, as though to engulf the itch with balm, the sweat glands started pumping. Within seconds, Lionel's black curly hair, not without a certain sheen at its best, was the waterlogged thatch of a man hoisted out of the Mersey.

Then he had noticed on the street one day men in business suits, with glistening hair. He had enquired. 'Wet look,' he'd been told. 'You should try Brilliant Gel.' So he had. And now, after massaging a quarter of a jar into his locks, he was free for the night. Already wet, he could get no wetter. Should he feel a dampness up above, he knew it could be ascribed to fashion instead of sexual panic. He walked in to the bar.

'Raining again, is it?' the barman asked, looking at Lionel's doused tonsure.

'*Au contraire*,' Jason said brightly. Some people simply didn't keep up with the trends.

At that moment Sylvie lay on her little sofabed in the corner of her room at the Signum, sound asleep. When she woke it was to the sound of John Lennon's voice, issuing from the throat of a bull. A man with a bull's head. Slowly this sound transmuted to the horn of a ship making its way down the Mersey. It took her a second to remember who and where she was. Then she looked at her watch. Ten-past eight. Tom.

She renovated her face with a little powder, kohl and blusher. Her green eyes, normally so sharp, had a vague look about them. Five minutes later she was there. Tom was already sitting at a table, book in hand, with a glass of white wine before him. They traded hellos.

'Wine?'

'Don't think I could face any to be honest. The bouquet's still hanging around from last night.'

'Feeling a bit foggy, are you? I have the perfect cure.'

'Do you?'

'Yes, as long as you don't ask any questions and just trust me.' Sylvie couldn't be bothered thinking about anything any more. Done enough thinking for one week. 'All right then.'

The drink he put before her was entirely colourless and entirely still.

'What is it?'

'Remember the agreement. No questions. Drink it.' So she did. And he was right, it did make her feel better almost immediately, though there was obviously some spirit in it. She didn't care. They started to talk. Soon their drinks were finished. She offered to buy a round but that would have involved the disclosure of what she was drinking, so he got it instead. By the time she had finished the second glass she felt considerably better; in fact quite lively. She now joined him in a glass of white wine. Red wine was Henry, Shropshire, the Riverside Gallery, minotaurs and pizzas. White seemed freer of any unwanted heaviness. Half-way through it she remembered she hadn't eaten all day.

'Let's go down to the Everyman,' he said, which suited her because it always had vegetarian quiches and various salads. As she came through the door on to the pavement outside she stumbled slightly, and he put his hand on her back to steady her. Then he kept it there. He was almost a foot taller than she was, taller even than Owen. A good rudder if a girl needed guiding.

'What were those drinks? Am I allowed to know now?'

'Vodka and water. Still water. Delicious isn't it? Cleanest drink on earth.' In fact they'd both been doubles. At the Everyman he ordered a large carafe of white wine. They ate; they drank; they talked. Sylvie was soon asking herself how she had missed this character. The Signum had a relationship of affiliation to the University. All sorts of things involving the awarding of degrees, validation of courses, entry requirements, and there was a fair deal of coming and going between them. She'd heard of Tom, heard that he was a very well-informed scientist, with a tremendous following at his lectures. Though what was it Alison had said about him? She couldn't be bothered thinking about it. For the moment, as he seemed to connect with all her main concerns, she found herself growing livelier and livelier. They really would have to start seeing more of each other; he filled her glass again.

'I'm not sure what the impact of the things you're talking about has been in science. We still tend to be all too trusting of images. I try to point out to my colleagues that whatever the

Hubble images are they're certainly not snapshots in space – these are constructed photographs. A lot of construction goes into them, and I often wonder if the aesthetic constraint isn't at least as strong as the observational one. But you were talking about how modernity subverts itself. Duchamp's urinal. Dada.' Sylvie took another sip of her drink before replying.

'I'm intrigued by things a little nearer to home. In fact, things around the corner. How in the 60s these new stars were first put on pedestals and then tried very hard to throw themselves off them. *Magical Mystery Tour* didn't really come off. But have you seen *Don't Look Back* or *Eat the Document?*' He shook his head. 'I've got copies of them at the Signum, one of them not strictly legal, but never mind. There was a resistance to absorption in the corporate world of advertising and promotion, which can still shock. It did seem at one point as if Dylan would simply explode. The commodity that exploded.' She smiled at her own phrase, which she had never used before. 'When Godard made *One Plus One*, he wouldn't play the whole of the song, which pissed the Stones off, though he pissed them off anyway. But I can understand why. It's a pretty terrible film looking back, Godard at his nastiest, but he didn't want to fulfil expectations in that way.'

'So what happened?' He was filling her glass again. Why did she not always drink white wine? It hardly seemed to have any effect on her at all.

'It didn't work. It seems that the image, even when it's subverting itself, still manages to reinforce its transcendent reality at the same time. This was one of Euland's greatest fears. He said that the power of self-critical analysis can never keep up with the amplification of the modern image. We have created a culture in which we are overwhelmed by our own images, and there seems to be no escape. We're trapped inside the corridors of our own endless gallery of images.'

'It sounds like a labyrinth.' She started laughing.

'You're right, Tom. It sounds like a labyrinth. Though don't ask me who's the minotaur and who's the virgin.' At which point he put his hand on her thigh. And she left it there. No rules any more. She was going to have to make up a new set quickly.

'Are you married, Tom?'

'Getting divorced.'

'That makes two of us.'

'We could share notes. Don't believe everything you hear about me, by the way.'

'Do you have somewhere to go?'

'Not my house. My wife and child are there. Things are getting sorted out, but not quite yet.'

'Well, we certainly can't go back to the Signum.'

'Why not? I heard you stay over there sometimes.'

'By myself. With Hamish lurking around . . . God, I can't even bear to think about it.'

'We can be quiet.'

Sober, Sylvie would never have done it, but she was far from sober. The two double vodkas on an empty stomach, then all the wine, probably more than a litre, since Tom had been more attentive to her needs than his own. Plus the odd sense of exhilaration as it occurred to her more and more vividly that she was free. She had told Owen to go and it seemed that he'd done as he was told. And she had not spent the night with Henry, because he had accepted her farewell, and put her in the spare bedroom instead. So she wasn't sleeping around, was she? If anything, she was doing the opposite of that. She owed no one anything and she'd been not far off a nun for the last few years. And she did like Tom. Something about both his intellect and his body appealed to her this evening.

As they left the pub she spotted Lionel, wet-headed and solitary.

'Out chasing women?' she asked him.

'*Au contraire.*'

Five minutes later they made their way up the creaking steps of the Signum, tiptoed down the corridor, and shuffled in to Sylvie's room with only the mildest of giggles.

'You'll have to leave early. Before Hamish is up and about.'

'I'll go first thing.'

So much of sex is politeness. That was in one of Owen's scripts, she remembered, but she could never remember which one. Tom was very polite at the beginning. Decorous, responsive, making sure she liked each stage. She did. His body, taut and agile, was such a change from Henry. A lot more like Owen, in fact, though less angular, less . . . she didn't know less what. Then he became less polite, but by then that was what she wanted him to be. She called out his name in the darkness.

When she woke up, he had already gone. There was a note on the table. *I'll phone you. Love, Tom.* She remembered who and where she was briefly, and then decided she had better get back to Chester before she remembered any more. She wanted a quick shower. She stepped out on to the corridor and saw Hamish sitting on a wooden chair, reading a book. He looked up at her, unsmiling.

'Ms. Ashton, as I believe you are now called, I think you and I need to have a serious talk at some point about the nature of this institution.' She could think of nothing at all to say, so walked in silence down to the bathroom.

The Motel Route to Wisdom

The book that lay open on the floor next to the makeshift bed where Alex Gregory slipped in and out of consciousness recounted the long travail that had been Lady Pneuma's life in America when she first proclaimed her gospel: the motels, the manicured greensward rising to the shopping mall, diners with their burgers, fizzing drinks, heavily-gutted men draped in white aprons. A world shaped into a prophylactic against her seminal words. She spoke at length about cars. Cars, the endless lines of cars in their liturgical processions, back and forth to the mighty urban shrines. For what? The flashing shrines with their truckloads of secular treasure. Moloch and Mammon, in a dizzy waltz, with a neon Christ perched on the top, a shining decoration, no more, his crucified body curving now like a dollar sign.

Science she proclaimed a degenerate form of art, which had replaced song with measurement and had forgotten in any case that all counting ended in infinity. Its humble function had been to describe our location; instead it had usurped the sacred wisdom. Good and evil, she explained, are recently invented categories, brought in to explain why all the causes cannot cohere; and thereby enable us to fathom why there is contrariety and tension in the force-field of the world. What Pneuma had noted more and more in her study of the goddess was that she who gives birth also slaughters. Astarte, Medea. But these are the takers of flesh, even the eaters of flesh; they enter the flesh of the gods and are entered by it. Not so with Mary. She is entered once and once only, by the Spirit. It is air itself then that enters her, and the god who then exits.

It was a Taoist doctrine that evil, seeing its own image in the mirror, would promptly destroy itself, unable to countenance the horror that was its own identity. One day Pneuma had looked in the mirror and found nothing there at all; no engrossed dark matter. Then she knew the real journey had begun. But it had still taken the intervention in her life of Hermann Gebler to launch her world-wide movement. Gebler was technically her husband, though as she explained in her introduction, this term could be no more than a flag of convenience, given that any possibility of fleshly union had already been transcended. It was Gebler who had seen her charismatic potential; he who had formed the Delta Foundation, published *The One True Elemental*, and gone on to produce the videos, arrange the elusive tours, distribute the hagiographic vignettes. Her book was dedicated to him, and the goddess.

This book lay face-down on the floor as Alex's body began its emaciated journey into hypothermia. She was seriously weakened now by four weeks of inanition. She was also radically dehydrated since she had drunk nothing for three days. When she occasionally surfaced into consciousness she felt a sharp dryness in her throat which would have made her retch, but there was nothing inside her to retch with. Her chest had a stone weight upon it. She felt as though each organ inside her were being eaten by acid. Could this finally be the beginning of enlightenment?

Doll's House

Sylvie was hoping she didn't have to see Hamish again for a while. She needed a little solidarity. So when she heard Alison's door open, she waited two minutes then slipped across quickly to see her.

'Hello Sylvie. How's things?'

'A bit complicated really.' Sylvie was staring at the large poster which Alison had pinned to her wall. It showed a gleaming sculpture by the Italian artist Rembrandt Bugatti. Alison had been to the exhibition in London a few years before.

'Rembrandt Bugatti. Now there's a name to make you pause.'

'Bet you can't think of anyone else with the surname of a famous artist followed by a famous car?'

'Bacon Rolls?' Alison smiled; Sylvie didn't. Alison was three inches smaller than Sylvie, who wasn't very tall herself. This meant that Alison was the only person in the Institute Sylvie could look down on. Alison was even more hunched than normal. All the tension in her body, in her life, seemed to congregate in the middle of her shoulders. Her head seemed to be trying to disappear into her spine. Sylvie constantly had the urge to get hold of her by the neck, and pull her upright in a single jerk. There now, that's better, isn't it?

'So what's going on?'

'You won't get angry with me, will you?'

'No.'

'Promise?'

'I promise.'

'I told Owen I want a divorce.'

'Why should I get angry with you for that? The only question there is why it took you so long.'

'That's not all. Do you remember the bloke I mentioned to you in Shrewsbury – the one with the Picassos?'

'The one who was twenty years older than you and was letting his waistband out as he grew more spherical?'

'That's the one. Well, he asked me to marry him this week.'

Alison started laughing. 'Can I guess the answer?'

'The thing is . . . I had slept with him from time to time. I didn't really think of it as an affair, to be honest.'

'More of a sleep-over.'

'More of a monthly sleep-over. I mean he's very sweet and always very nice to me and . . . Oh God, Alison.'

'Made a change from Owen, I should think. Which I daresay you needed. No harm done, is there, and I should think he got his money's worth, knowing you.'

'Owen could be sweet when it suited him, you know. Let's not start slagging off men.'

'Why not? They spend half their lives slagging off women.'

'Anyway, there's something else.'

'Christ, Sylvie, where do you get your energy? Not surprised you haven't finished your book.' Sylvie took a deep breath.

'Last night I slept with Tom Helsey.' For the first time Alison's lips tightened. Any trace of a smile now disappeared. Her head seemed to ratchet one more inch down into her spine.

'Are you out of your mind?'

'I couldn't remember what you said about him exactly . . . I mean I'd had a few drinks.'

'Did he tell you he was getting divorced?' Now Sylvie's lips tightened.

'Yes. I mean, he *is* getting divorced.'

'No, he isn't, but that's his line. I've been told. He's already worked his way through all the old slappers over in the science block, so now he's moving in on the Signum, is he? He only shifted his attention to the staff because it was made plain to him by the powers-that-be over there that if he fucked another student, he'd be out. Where did you do it?'

'Here.' Alison's small delicate features now registered a distaste intensified by incredulity.

'HERE?'

'And Hamish . . . seems to know all about it.' Alison put her hand to her face.

'We're almost quorate, you know, to bring a vote of no confidence against that poisonous dwarf . . . ' – who was, Sylvie couldn't help noting, several inches taller than Alison herself – 'I do hope you're not going to wobble, Sylvie. Because if you do, you'll find you don't have many friends around here.'

*

Henry Allardyce sat surrounded by minotaurs and told himself that he knew, and had always known really, that it could never have worked out. Actually he told his third wife this, since he had taken her photograph out of the drawer where he had lain it face-down after he had started his affair – was that the right word? – with Sylvie. They'd slept together no more than twenty times. Was that an affair, or merely a take-away pizza service, with some accommodation thrown in? Had he behaved like a doting older man? He had, hadn't he?

'I suppose I just needed a little comfort, darling. Don't hold it against me. You don't, do you?' The image in the photograph uttered no complaint, so he took that as a no. 'She was very attractive. No more attractive than you, of course. But then you haven't walked through my door for such a long time, have you? And she did, that's all.' The serene smile of the third, and by far the sanest, of Henry's spouses assured him that he need feel no guilt. He might accuse himself of a little emotional folly, if he so chose, but guilt was unnecessary. He found this comforting. He put the photograph back into place on the table and picked up the invitation that had landed on his mat.

Henry Allardyce
is invited to the opening of
Dressmaker
by Miriam French

He was hardly ever interested in the things put on by that gallery in town. The last one – *Everything's Untrue Except the Dog* – had left him bored and baffled. But today he felt like getting out. He would lock up the gallery and walk in to Shrewsbury. He would see the exhibition, might even have a late lunch at that wine bar at the top of the hill, having checked the art section of the Oxfam bookshop. Cheer up, lads, he said to the minotaurs on the walls. You can't lose what you never owned in the first place.

Dressmaker. In the centre of the floor was an old doll's house, a big Edwardian-looking one, and all around it, forming queues to each door, were files of miniature dressmaker's dummies on their monopod metal stands, each one tarnished with age. All the clothes on the dummies were distressed, cut or torn, and some had flashes of red satin showing through like tiny rivulets of blood. Some still had their pins sticking out at curious angles from unexpected places. Henry found it oddly moving. He normally avoided anything to which the name 'installation' could be attached, but he kept walking round and round. Fragments of old newspapers had been pasted on to the doll's house, dating from the time of the First World War, and it took him a moment to realise that the torn headlines, if you read them in sequence, spelt out: *Dressing ourselves in one another's wounds*. And then when you peered through the windows of the little house you saw those photographs, the heartrending photographs from the trenches. Men slumped over their rifles, smoking. Men with bandages on legs or heads or arms, or everywhere.

'What do you think, Henry?' This was Maria, the gallery-owner. He knew her voice so well he didn't even turn around.

'I think it's beautiful, Maria, honestly. Not sure what it is, exactly, but I'd be happy to be holding this exhibition at my gallery.'

'Then let me introduce you to the artist, Miriam French.' Henry turned around and saw the tall woman in a white trouser-suit. Her hair was either blonde or bleached and it had been cropped to within a quarter of an inch of her skull. Her eyes were aquamarine. In her heels she was a good six inches taller than Henry, and she stared down at him smiling.

'Miriam, this is Henry Allardyce. Riverside Galleries. Remember, I told you about him.'

'You have the Picassos. The *Vollard Suite*. Some of my favourite pictures in the world, but I've only seen most of them in reproduction. Any chance I could come over and have a look?'

'Why not? When did you want to come?'

'I'm going back to London tomorrow. Would this evening be any good?'

'Fine. About seven-thirty. You know where to come?'

'I'll give her directions, Henry.'

So Henry didn't go to the wine bar. He went to Marks and Spencer instead and bought various salads, and a large pizza. Vegetarian, just in case. A couple of bottles of decent red wine, then he went back home and put his wife's photograph away again. Could it really be that one door was opening as another closed?

'This is ridiculous,' he said to himself. She couldn't be any older than Sylvie. Calm down, Henry. It's Picasso's bull's horns she wants to examine closely, not yours.

But in fact the evening was not ridiculous; it was remarkably pleasant. And it became evident to Henry early on that any hint of physicality was out of the question. He couldn't work out why he was so sure of this; certainly not any lack of attraction on his part. Then Miriam spoke of her partner in London, and once, instead of saying partner, she said Sue. Now we've got that out of the way, thought Henry, we might as well enjoy ourselves.

'Do you like pizza?'

'Love it.'

'Would you be vegetarian, by any chance?'

'How did you know?'

'Just a hunch. I can spot female vegetarians at fifty paces. I'm often responsible for saving them from starvation. Shropshire can be a harsh environment for herbivores.'

And for the rest of the evening, Henry gave her the benefit of his considerable knowledge about the *Vollard Suite*. She really did want to know, and he had the knowledge she needed. Once every few months a busload of students from one Shropshire school or another would turn up by arrangement, and Henry would give them a lecture for half an hour. He didn't need notes. Miriam often sprang up from her chair, and looked closely at some detail of one of the etchings. As she observed the pictures, he observed her. Not for the first time in his life, he thought it might be a shame he wasn't a woman.

As she was leaving she said, 'Thank you so much. It's been delightful, it really has. I can't tell you what it's meant to me to sit there all evening with those Picassos. If I come back here one day with my partner, would you mind if we both landed on you for a couple of hours?'

'You're more than welcome, at any time.' He meant it too. 'Give me enough notice to buy the pizza. Sue a vegetarian too, is she?' Miriam nodded. 'I know how you all tend to stick together.'

'You should have Maria over some time, you know. She'd appreciate it.'

'Can't stand her husband, unfortunately.'

'Neither can she now. He's gone. Hadn't you heard? Shacked up with some twenty year-old piece of skirt in London. Shouldn't think that'll last long.'

She stopped and turned back towards him when she reached the gate.

'Do you think I might be able to do something with it? This labyrinth theme?'

'Everybody else is. But just remember, when you're in the labyrinth, you're marked for death.'

'What if you're out of the labyrinth?' Henry thought for a moment.

'You're still marked for death.'

'Then it sounds like six of one and half a dozen of the other to me.'

Nudes

That was the title of one of Sylvie's more popular lectures.

She normally started with Walter Sickert, a painting called *Le Lit de Cuivre*. The woman naked on the bed is only half-emerging from the murk, as though the world of Edwardian England is simply not ready for the openly naked body, as though the rotting fabric of the *zeitgeist* clings about the portrayal of nudity so as to properly obscure it. Then it was back to nineteenth-century Paris: Toulouse-Lautrec, Degas, Rodin. The nude of the brothel; the nude of the rub-down; the nude of athletic sexuality. For once Lionel's eyes weren't fixed on her legs. There was a minor detour then through Alma-Tadema – the nude as a spurious exemplum of antiquity. Stimulation as scholarship. The aesthete's eye as the camera lens of the pornographer. On to Klimt: Viennese corruption, a gilded invitation card slipped inside a silk chemise, followed by Egon Schiele: sex in the sanatorium, sex as tubercular derangement. One or two slides of Ingres' orientalist fantasies of nubile women spread over richly woven eastern carpets. A few versions of Andromeda; and one of George and the Dragon. You didn't have to be schooled as an expert in the workings of the psyche to appreciate the significance of a man stiff in his armour approaching a naked young woman chained to a rock. Not everyone's idea of a good time on a Saturday night, but archetypal all the same.

Then she would confront them with Stanley Spencer and his double portraits with that monster of subterfuge and duplicity, Patricia Preece. She explained how this woman had consumed the artist, brutally, heartlessly, with malice aforethought. His innocence was nutritious enough for her to feed upon for the rest of her life. These paintings somehow prefigured that consumption. She edged towards Francis Bacon: sex as rage, a howl against the void and then, once she was sure they were ready for it, and Lionel wouldn't pass out, Lucian Freud.

She had also come to show more and more slides of Bonnard. He had painted such a clutch of pictures of a woman in a bath that she'd assumed it must be some sort of obsession with him: the oceanic feeling? Primal urges still surging inside us from our distant aquatic origins? But then she read a biography and discovered that Bonnard's wife Marthe so entirely divided the day between the bed and the bath that she was effectively amphibian. So if he was going to employ wifey as an unpaid model (though he paid for her in other respects, that was for sure) then he didn't have much choice except to paint her in the bath. (She had made a note to herself: what is the long-term effect of steam on oil-paints while they're being applied to canvas? The same as on the glue of an envelope? Might Bonnard's paint already be peeling away from those pre-moistened surfaces? She must ask Henry. He'd surely know.)

He tended to avoid portraying Marthe's feet. Had she become so hydrophilic that they were webbed?

Then finally Picasso. She would introduce the matter with some spurious illustrations. A sketch of a woman flamboyantly pleasuring herself, legs well apart; Picasso being fellated by one of his many mistresses. Artistically worthless, undoubtedly, but they always captured the attention. Then on to the *Vollard Suite*. She had learnt a great deal from Henry's informal tutorials. But she had also noticed things for herself. She had given as well as taken; it wasn't as though she had anything to feel guilty about with Henry. In Picasso the women are always bathed in the gaze of the artist, as though that is all that keeps them alive: the gaze of the artist, the touch of the minotaur. In Bonnard though, as in Degas, the women seem entirely disconnected, in a separate world, another existence into which the artist has silently intruded. They are not models either, as Picasso's invariably seemed to be, even if he happened to be married to them at the time. They are always doing something, thinking something, undergoing sorrows the artist cannot touch or redeem. They cannot be captured, they are for ever looking away or beyond. Their activities, even merely lying in a bath, are by way of an emphasis upon that melancholy state of separation and division between the seeing eye and the creature seen.

Then she'd noticed something else: in most of Bonnard's self-portraits the eyes seem almost closed, painted out to a hollow as though exhausted from the grief of looking, even though it is those same eyes which give us the image and even though the colours themselves speak of nothing but joy. But they themselves are blank, blind and blank, as if the paint of the world has come off on them from too much looking. As though they'd been blinded by the scrupulous detailing of too many rainbows.

But Picasso's eyes are whatever is the opposite of blind. He was proud of his *mirada fuerta*, that gaze which possesses what it lands upon. Those eyes are all-consuming. Leo Stein said that after he'd given Picasso some engravings to look at, the Spaniard stared at them with such intensity that by the time he'd finished it seemed surprising there'd been any marks left on the paper at all.

And how did she finish? With a photograph. A photograph of what appeared to be an object fashioned 250,000 years ago on what we now call the Golan Heights. Female, apparently. Crude enough, for sure; it wasn't about to win any National Portrait Gallery awards. It was a piece of stone scraped with tools until it had taken on the appearance of a fecund woman. Crude but potent. So it was made by a Neanderthal then, the creatures that our own ancestors, *homo sapiens*, had replaced, in whatever manner. What did this tell us? That from the very beginning in remaking the world in art we had recreated the world as a symbolic order. 'We bestow meaning by discovering creativity; we discover creativity by bestowing meaning. So there's our theme for today: art and sex, sex and art. From the Middle East of a quarter of a million years ago to the Signum Institute today, it is still more than simply a marriage of convenience.'

'Do you have any handouts for this lecture?' Lionel asked. How tall are you, Lionel, she wondered. If she sometimes felt parodically short, Lionel was more than parodic in the other direction. A gangling six and a half foot stringbean of sexual frustration and inadequacy. How many hours a night do you spend wrestling with the one-eyed python of desire, Lionel? She almost felt like performing the introductory rites herself, except that she could see Alison's hunched shoulders growing even more hunched, her menacing crouch of disapproval growing ever squatter. Why was his head always so soaked? Had he been dating a mermaid in the Mersey?

'Was it the illustrations you were particularly interested in?'

'They'd be great, yeah.'

'Well, they're all in the library, Lionel. There's even a few female librarians down there. So happy hunting.'

Claparède's Drawing-Pin

With the greatest reluctance, John Tamworth had agreed to
Owen's taking up residence in his flat.

'Only for a couple of weeks, Owen. I need my space.'

'We can work on this film.'

'We haven't actually got a film to work on yet.'

'I have.'

The flat in Chester overlooked the canal. You could almost
see St Clare's. Almost, but not quite. The rooms were like a
cinema museum, with all the posters on the wall, all the
books, all the old scripts. Row upon row of videos and DVDs
meant there was hardly a film you could name that wasn't
there somewhere, in one form or another. Owen loved it, but
he was aware that having him around all the time made John
uneasy. Having Owen around made a lot of people uneasy.
There was something about him, his inability to be still or let
things be, the fact that he never slept for longer than four or
five hours a night, that both intrigued and exhausted people.
With Johnny, intrigue had long ago given way to exhaustion,
but they still did their best work together. Whenever a Tamworth film came out without Treadle's name on it some critic
would be sure to point out that, sadly, it lacked the curious
electricity, that unexpected flicker and spark, they always
seemed to achieve whenever they worked together. They were
well and truly stuck with one another.

There was also the question of women. It wasn't that John

was excessively zipped-up in this respect; his wife lived in a house on the other side of town, with their two children. He went back there at weekends, usually anyway, though he made sure all the bills were paid. He had an intermittent relationship with the barmaid in a local pub, who had ambitions to be a film actress, ambitions which he suspected were very unlikely to be fulfilled. Everyone's life was complicated, he knew that, so he tended not to be moralistic about such things. It was just that with Owen something else came into play, something manic and uncontrollable; power assumed too great a part, the power of words over the power of bodies. And it alarmed him.

'Two weeks maximum, Owen, is that understood?' Owen nodded. 'Nothing personal, you understand. But I need this space to work in.'

'We're going to work. Can we look at the video footage from the other day . . . I don't want any sound.'

They had done this before, many times. And it had worked before, many times. 'Switch the other sound-recorder on.' So as they watched the images on the screen, Owen let the words begin. Free-associating. Saying whatever came into his mind. Most of it would be forgotten, it always was, but there was usually something there which they could use. He always seemed to find something he could get started on. He made John play the footage of the table over and over again, while he sat in silence staring at it, until the film-maker started to grow a little impatient. He simply couldn't see how there could be too much there of interest.

'For thirty years it's been here, this table, and its marks are its memory. As I stare down at its surface today, I realise it has more memory than I do. The marks inside me that you might call memory have all been erased. The table remembers its meals, its cigarette ends, its scorched rings from heated porcelain, but I can barely find the word for table. The table has been scored by its years, all the constellations of its events, and I've lost the marks, the shapes, the signs that form constellations inside me. I'm a blank sky. Black. A fresh sheet of formica. Grey. Except that it's all still in there somewhere . . . '

'So it's a first-person narrative?'

'Might be.'

'Constellations. That's one of Sylvie's things, isn't it? Better make sure she's properly acknowledged this time. She still reckons we ripped her off for all that art stuff we used when we made *In The Cave*'.

'She's probably right. Trouble is, I don't make a note of things I use. I take whatever I need.'

'I've noticed, Owen.'

'Let's look at the woman behind the counter again.' John wound the tape back. 'That doesn't need anything. Her image represents its own bewilderment. Let's look at the stuff on the road.' The images started to play, simultaneously haphazard and fluent as John moved the camera here and there. He usually had a Director of Photography for his work, but he was more than qualified to be his own Director of Photography when he chose. That was the route he'd arrived by.

'Sky. River. Estuary. Boat. Cloud. Speed. Sand. Quarry. These words come back into the mind like migrating birds that have been lost all winter. They fly across this sky without con-stellations, this sky that's starting to lighten now. There has been a siege in some lost time and townsfolk are making their way back one by one. Cut that – I don't like that . . . Start again. My mind is Lazarus, and it is stumbling out of the darkness to remind itself what happens in the light. Inside me are all the marks on the table, that tell me where there was heat or sharpness, pleasure or pain, but I still don't under-stand the signs.'

John played the footage from inside the room in the small hotel.

'I don't know whether these are my memories or someone else's, my images or someone else's, but they are crowding round now, like spectators at a crime-scene. I know that people have made love upon this bed, and that a man left here to go to a war, and that the woman he left behind had some mighty griefs to endure. Forthcoming griefs. But I don't know whether these images came naturally, or were manufactured.'

'How much do you remember, Owen?'

'More comes back every day. But there's still a lot left out. I think there might be one very big thing left out.'

And I think I know what it is, John thought. Might be better for you never to locate it. Alex Gregory. He re-played the images from the pier.

'And you stare and wonder, Do the boards have memories of all the feet that have walked over them? Do the iron railings remember the hundreds of thousands of fingers that have held them and stroked them? Do they remember sunshine and rain? Do the waves remember where they came from? Do ships remember their journeys, all the harbours they have entered and left? Am I the only one standing here without any traces of my own existence? So where did all the words come from then? All the words are there, it seems, and all the images are there too, but they've become disconnected.'

'Do we have a working title for this?' John asked when they had finished.

'Claparède's Drawing-Pin.'

'Explain.'

'1911. A Swiss psychiatrist called Claparède. Had a lot of patients suffering from anterograde amnesia. That's total memory wipe-out. One morning he hides a drawing-pin in his palm when he shakes hands with a female patient. The next day she won't shake hands with him. She didn't know who he was, couldn't remember him even coming before, but she wouldn't shake hands. Now we could call this the heart of the dilemma we have here: the relationship between implicit and explicit memory, how they relate and how they don't. What stays in there; what gets erased. I'm picking up the terminology from this book Sylvie leant me.' He held up the copy of *Amnesia*, a volume Sylvie had borrowed from the Signum.

'Something for you to remember her by. I'm still not sure I can see a film here. Are we talking about a thirty-minute number?'

'Don't know yet. Depends how far it all goes. Can you make the camera forget?'

'Forget what?'

'Everything. Is there some way of using filters or masks or something that lets us understand that the lens is starting to remember?'

'A lens remembers nothing, Owen.' And yet, as so often working with him, John Tamworth had at that moment seen a very interesting problem laid before him. Because of the way Owen did everything in words, these problems often seemed bizarre, even impossible, when they were first formulated. But then they often turned into something.

'You know what I mean, John. I can tell by that expression of yours, you know exactly what I mean. You always shake your head like that and say it's impossible when I give you something really interesting, like the cameraman on *Citizen Kane*. "Can't be done, Mr Welles; you can't shoot from that angle." We usually end up doing it, all the same, don't we? The lens has your memory – the way you point it and move it and choose focal lengths. I want you to think about using a lens as though you've never used one before, as though no one had ever used one before. Trying to find its depth of field, going in and out of focus. Moving in too close, going out too far. As though it was trying out the world for the first time, the way a man with anterograde amnesia has to find out where everything in the world is again. I'm telling you, with the right voice-over, it could be magical.'

And for the first time since all this had come up, John Tamworth began to believe that another film might have just got started between them.

It didn't make him like Owen Treadle any better.

Mirada Fuerte

With Owen inside it, the house had felt too small, much too small. Now it suddenly seemed very big. All those empty rooms. Not even a cat to prowl around, knocking things over. Should she phone Henry? The truth was that she would have liked to go and see Henry, right now. This particular evening she badly needed someone's company. Henry's gentle voice, gentle humour, nice wine, would all have been perfect. Why had she not simply let the relationship meander on? What harm would there have been in that, for either of them? But he wanted more than that, didn't he? And it wasn't fair to let him think there might be more than that, because there never would be. Some things couldn't be altered in life. She walked into the bathroom and stared at her face in the mirror. What a look of perplexity you seem to be rehearsing these days, Miss Ashton. Has Little Missey gone astray? No one to blame but yourself then, you old tart. She had tried to phone Tom Helsey four times and been connected to his answering machine on each occasion. Was that really his routine? A quick fuck and then fuck off? Was Alison right? She certainly seemed pretty confident about her facts. And can I really be so stupid at my age, to fall for that one? On the other hand, I was drunk. Talk about clutching at straws. Do some work, woman. Earn your keep. One last look in the mirror. Not bad, actually. All the anxiety had made her a fraction leaner.

Back to Picasso then. He so often turned his laughing women

into weeping women. Françoise Gilot put it thus: first you were the plinth, then the doormat. Women were either in the sky or on the floor. A woman weeps and the air about her fractures. She weeps and the tears turn into icicles or knives. She weeps and the room about her screams a vivid lament. Behind her a rainbow turns hysterical and spews out its colours. Van Gogh yellows bleed from the furniture. Soutine reds striate her face. A woman weeps until even her flesh is nothing but a serration of jagged edges. A shapely torso has turned overnight into a broken bottle. If you want to drink from it, it'll most likely be blood you'll be swallowing. So were these images a celebration of oppression or its truthful exposition? Could they have simply been a lament for the tragedies life affords? The tears had long ago dried, the salt stains vanished, but the paintings remain. Art, Lionel, lasts a lot longer than sex, but it's not always any less messy.

She turned and looked at the picture on her study wall. Always in all the photographs of him it is Picasso's eyes that dominate; they are lodestars – lodestones too, since they magnetised so many. Dark powers that led women to their salvation or doom, or often enough to both at the same time. *Mirada fuerte*, the strong gaze, devouring what it confronts. It exercised power over whatever came within its focus. Picasso was pursuing beauty all right but it had taken on different features, at times even becoming what we once called ugly. When Picasso showed him *Les Demoiselles D'Avignon*, even his close friend Braque said it was like drinking paraffin. Someone else said he'd end up hanged by the neck behind it. So he rolled it up and threw it underneath his bed, where it stayed for years, unknown and unlamented.

Sylvie looked at the photograph of Picasso on her wall and the photograph of Picasso looked back, the black pools of his eyes wide and deep enough, it seemed, to swallow a herd of thirsty elephants. So many memories down in the water. What was Henry's constant nightmare? The whole of the Renaissance drowned in the flood. The only eyes she knew anywhere near as dark as that were Owen's.

She left the room and went downstairs to the telephone. John answered.

'Is everything all right?'

'I suppose so. Will he be coming back to you when it's all over?'

'Don't think so, Johnny. Not this time. Not after . . . well, you know. I was thinking of coming over your way to that little Italian place. Fancy a bite? Just the three of us? Be like old times.'

'Let me ask Owen.' She could hear a brief conversation, then he was back. 'That's fine. Say half an hour?'

They sat together at the table in silence for a few minutes, then Owen started laughing. Owen had a winning laugh; it swooped, levitated, settled on unexpected objects. John joined in, and then Sylvie.

'Why are we laughing?' she said finally.

'Why not?'

The waiter came over to the laughing table.

'Can I take your order?'

'I know what I want,' Owen said. 'Pasta penne.'

'I'll have the Bolognese,' John said.

'Can I ask what's in the vegetarian pizza?' Sylvie asked. The waiter shrugged.

'Lots of vegetables.'

'Fair enough. I'll have that then.'

'White wine or red?'

'I'll stick with water tonight,' Sylvie said.

'Red all right, Owen? We'll have a carafe of the red.'

'How's your mother, by the way?' John asked and Owen smiled.

'You're so good at pleasantries, John.' Why did Owen look so attractive tonight? Was it because he was on his way out of her life, or was it that his new-found freedom had lit him up? His *mirada fuerte* was blazing. Wouldn't have too much trouble picking up some young piece around Chester, but then he never did have much trouble, did he?

'She's not too bad, thanks, John. Still studying her Krishnamurti, trying to make the many one.'

'Who isn't?' Owen asked.

'I don't think I am,' John said. 'I think I prefer the one to be many. Like George Oppen I believe in the shipwreck of the singular.'

'You met him once, didn't you? Krishnamurti.'

'Yes. I think I must have been about sixteen. There was some huge marquee, I remember that, and all these crowds of hushed and excited people wandering about. We managed to get a seat up near the dais. And after what seemed hours the little man came out, dressed like a landowner from the pages of *Country Life*, in a nicely-cut tweed jacket and cavalry twills. He spoke for so long I finally dozed off. I remember a lot of phrases like "Not to be in love with something but simply to be in love, in the state of it." But for as long as I was awake I couldn't take my eyes off his hair.

'As she drove me back later my mother seemed torn between her new state of spiritual elevation, and her disgruntlement with her feckless daughter. "You fell asleep," she said. "How could you do that?" "Because I was tired," I said. "You can get tired any time. It's not every day you get to see Krishnamurti. See him, be in his presence, listen to his wisdom." "So why does he do that with his hair then, if he's so wise?" "What?" "Come on, mother, don't tell me you didn't notice. He kept going on about there being no secrets that can be kept from the questing spirit, so why does he go to all that trouble to comb his white hair over his bald patch? You can see it from a mile away; you don't have to be on the astral plane. So why's he so desperate to keep that a secret then?"

'My mother never quite forgave me for that. If it had been me in the burning building and Krishnamurti, she'd definitely have saved him and left me for cinders. Left me to find a spiritual purging in the flames. Not like your mother, eh Owen?'

'No, with mine it was Jesus all the way.'

'So she went round forgiving people all the time, did she?'

'On the contrary, she thought the forgiveness side of things in Christianity had been seriously over-promoted. She was keen to emphasize the other side of Jesus: maledictions on fig trees, booting money-lenders out of the temple. Get thee behind me, Satan.

'Actually, to be fair, there were only two things my mother absolutely couldn't stand: unpunctuality and sinners. But then since nobody is always exactly on time, and only Jesus and his mother lived a life entirely without sin, what this actually amounted to was that my mother never liked anyone much. Not for long anyway. She certainly never liked me. Every so often she might tilt a little towards one endearing soul or another, but soon enough he'd turn up five minutes late, or be spotted talking to a member of the opposite sex in an unregulated zone, and that would be his name erased for ever from the book of life. Found it hard now to fathom what she'd ever seen in him in the first place. A man so slovenly he couldn't even set his watch; a fornicator soliciting strangers he encountered at the kerbside. Another foot-soldier in the devil's army, desperate and woe-begone. "We'll still be keeping him as our doctor though, won't we, Mum?" I'd ask, desperate for a bit of continuity. "We'll keep him as our doctor for the moment, until a more spiritually salubrious practitioner turns up.'''

'Why was she like that?' John always had to find the reason behind things; he never believed anything could be arbitrary.

'My Dad, I suppose. The old man had a fish and chip shop in Swansea. He also had a penis that never stayed zippered for more than ten hours at a time. Took a couple of years after they were married before Mum realised what had been going on. It was one night when he'd taken the dog for a walk. Used to go down around the graveyard. Mum didn't like it down there. Thought it was creepy. That's probably why he went. Very long walks, that dog used to get. Anyway the dog came back this time, minus Dad. So Mum went off on a search for once. Went to the pub, obvious first port-of-call, but he wasn't there. Finally galvanized herself to go down to the graveyard, and spotted Dad, up against one of the larger catacombs, having a knee-trembler with a local floozie. That's when she took to the Gospel in earnest.'

'You never told me that, Owen.'

'Didn't I? Probably thought you were too young in those days.'

'I've aged, obviously.' So are you a chip off the old block, my husband? Is it no more than the inescapability of genetics? Or was that the choice you thought life had presented you with, Bible-thumping or fornication? Why had he never told her about his father? She'd even met the old fellow. Was he still at it, down in Swansea? Or had he finally achieved a state of senile detumescence?

The odd thing was, when the evening finally came to a close, she wanted to go back with them both to John's flat. She didn't want to sleep with either of them, only to lie on a separate bed and talk into the small hours. Without being touched. Was that such an unreasonable request? Didn't seem to be one that could be fulfilled, anyway, so she didn't bother making it.

Marks of Light

Henry had taken out the photographs of all his wives now, and laid them across the table in the Picasso Room.

He picked up one of his first wife Isabella, lying on the beach, her eyes shut. It made him think of her when she was sleeping: she was such a tidy, regulated sort of a person. Only at night did curious sighs and coded signals start to escape from her mouth. So many complaints. A murmurous little riot between the sheets. The hermetic protest her soul permitted itself while Isabella's daytime mind was on the blink. When the god of money finally closed his eyes. She had creatures locked inside her who never saw the light of day. So when her mind had been switched off, when these hidden creatures could wander at last through the deserted playground of her spirit, so many dead streets left vacant in the hours of darkness, they all spoke at once in urgent whispers. Henry used to lie there and listen, fascinated, beguiled. He'd wanted to meet them; wanted to run a phrenological hand across their little skulls to locate the bumps, so that he might map the miniature topographies of their souls. But come the morning they would all be safely locked away once more inside the businesswoman's brain. Isabella of course simply denied their existence.

In the photographs of Laura, she was always provocative, but then in this particular instance, the photographs were merely recording reality. In one she had started to pull the T-shirt up over her breasts, and as Henry recalled, he hadn't spent much longer with his eye to the viewfinder.

And then Eleanor. Eleanor simply smiled. Whatever happened to her, she smiled. You didn't have to ask Eleanor to smile, because she was already doing it. So much pain in her life; so many smiles.

He seemed to spend more and more hours alone in the Picasso Room. What separate worlds Picasso's men and women inhabit. They even look at each other in different languages. Light a candle in your heart, Henry, and trim its wick in solitude. Let the wounded minotaur retire into his labyrinth.

Go out for a walk, man. And so he did. He stopped when he reached the pub by the river. Should it be a pint by the water-front, watching the Severn go by? That seemed like a good idea. Hadn't had a glass of wine all day; he'd wanted one, but he'd run out, and couldn't be bothered going out to buy any more. He sat down next to two young men, with close-cropped skulls. Neither of you can carry off the skinhead style like Miriam French, he thought, but he kept his thought to himself. One of the young men was talking in low, urgent tones.

'I'm going to kill that fucking dog of his, if it does it again in my garden.' The other's voice became quieter.

'They're tooled-up.'

'Tooled-up?'

'Armed.'

'Ah.'

'They don't bring their work home with them, like. Not so as I've heard. But I think it might be better if you don't mention about killing his dog. He might get a bit touchy about that.'

'Just go down the pet shop and get myself a pooper-scooper, you mean?'

'Might be the best idea, to be honest.'

'You're probably right.'

And the Severn rolled on. It had seen off the Romans. It'll see us off as well, Henry thought. With our dogs beside us. All our dead drowned dogs beside us, as we make for the exit.

When Henry arrived home that night he went and looked in the mirror. What he saw was very much not Pablo Picasso. For one thing he had more hair than Picasso, and he was taller. But there was no *mirada fuerte*, no facility for bewitching the beloved object.

'Can you not resign yourself to sharing the sheets with no one?' Henry asked himself. He didn't hear any answer so he went and sat in the Picasso Room until he fell asleep.

Genius

Sylvie had prepared her lecture. She had to make a real effort now to set off to the Institute. She was counting the days until the end of term. She was doing everything in her power to avoid Hamish. There had been no call from Tom Helsey. Down she went through the tunnel, with a million tons of water overhead. Even the radio cut out.

She sat cross-legged on the table before them. She had her jeans on so Lionel had nothing to really focus on and was looking out of the window.

'Geniuses. They have become an indispensable requirement of modernity, and often the main protagonists in our hunt for the significance of life. Part psychopomp, those figures who walk ahead and lead us to the Underworld, and part shaman to climb up the *axis mundi* and re-locate us in the centre of reality, they do some of our living, much of our thinking, and a great deal of our creating for us. In the world of show-business they are sometimes expected to suffer and die on our behalf too, like briefly glamorized redeemers. I've shown you that image of the minotaur, bewildered and defeated as the spectators look on. Well imagine John Lennon in the street in New York, with all the bullets in his body, stumbling backwards as the spectators stare.

'Let's look at two images for our purposes this morning. One is a picture of scientific genius and one of artistic genius. We might find they have more in common as part of our world-view than we would imagine.'

She switched on the overhead projector and slid the first image into place.

'This image of Einstein with electrodes attached to his head has come to symbolise the mysterious fact of genius, the unquantifiable sprite that's locked away inside the cerebellum. In an essay in his book *Mythologies* Roland Barthes pondered the meaning of this photograph. While all the wires linked Einstein up to his monitoring machinery, he'd been asked to think of relativity. This was presumably to send the maximum pulse waves coursing down the lines. The implication was clearly that, for the rest of us, thinking might emit a relatively meagre electro-magnetic signal, but when Einstein really got down to it, the intellect re-arranged every single force-field around it. The iconographic implication of the image seems to me more significant: we are being presented with the idea of genius as *magical interiority*. The shadowed world we inhabit is about to be illuminated by the gleaming singularity of Albert Einstein's mind. Time, place and circumstance are irrelevant, as this reproduction of the scene of thought in a laboratory many years later and elsewhere clearly indicates. The freakishly charged individual, intellectually potent beyond expectation, engages with the world and re-creates it for our understanding. But the facts of the matter are quite different.' Come on Lionel, stop looking out of the bloody window; I'm trying to tell you something important here. Should have worn my skirt, shouldn't I: then at least his head would be pointing in the right direction.

'The truth is that Einstein's intellectual development is inseparable from his time and circle: inseparable from his mathematics teacher Josef Zametzer, for example, and his Uncle Jakob, who was involved professionally with the latest electrotechnology, and was much in evidence as the partner of Einstein's father in a joint business they both ran in Munich. There was also the poor

Jewish student Max Talmey, who lent the youthful Einstein popular guides to science. What becomes even more striking in retrospect, as Galison shows so clearly, is that his work at the Berne Patent Office, apart from offering the young physicist the intellectual leisure he was later to joke about, also provided him with material for his work on relativity. He was dealing with lots of applications for patents relating to the co-ordination of time-signals. His genius came out of his implication in the world; not his dissociation from it. Relativity was a conceptual response to a set of contemporary problems. What Einstein proved was that all local times were valid, since neither space nor time could be assigned an absolute value. It was a question of fully under-standing the rules of conversion from one context to another.

'We work in the context where we find ourselves. None of this is to deny that Einstein had genius; it is only to try to understand what genius is and how it works, and how we form images of it. Our first caveman could constellate, remember, but he couldn't constellate a plough, because he hadn't made one yet. But take one last look at the image. What it is telling us is that the light shines from within. It will illuminate the dark outside.

'Now if the disshevelled, beslippered, pipe-smoking dis-traction of Einstein's baggy features meant scientific genius for the last century, the face of Picasso undoubtedly came to mean its artistic counterpart. A vulgar detestation of Cubism and Surrealism undoubtedly helped promote him as the manic Spanish dwarf of what is known to so many as modern art. Picasso became the emblematic figure of artistic genius for our time, as Einstein became the image of the scientific variety. A single vignette of their faces is enough to signify their meaning: their physiognomies are so potent, words are not required. Their appearances have become signs.

'Picasso, with that special stare of his, is about to transform reality. In one film he even paints with light. The same magical interiority is at work, since Picasso had neither a visible subject nor, it appeared, even a visible medium. Not even canvas or a lump of clay. Because we become one with the medium of the film in the process of watching it, the film itself as a medium gives the impression of being nothing at all, or at least being merely the medium of our thoughts; it is the materialisation of insubstantiality. Like the ether which Poincaré retained and Einstein discarded, its substance is hypothetical. Picasso creates out of nothing then, *ex nihilo*, precisely as God was said to do by orthodox theology. Einstein had already established that nothing in the universe could move faster than the speed of light, so the fact that Picasso could make images, and most compelling images too, out of light itself moving freely through the air from a torch in his hand, with nothing to prompt him but his own bright interiority, meant that his artistic spirit travelled as speedily as anything in creation ever could. He was spirit then, that *ruah* or *pneuma* of the first page of Genesis: *And the Spirit of God moved upon the face of the waters. And God said, Let there be light: and there was light.* In the relative world of mundanity, he had reached the actual speed of creation. The photons of genius were being emitted from him, and we were left behind to study their traces, since we are unable to travel with the same velocity.

'There was a long tradition before modern optics really began with Newton, which interpreted vision as coming from inside; we projected a light upon the objects we saw. The light then was referred to as *lux*, not the *lumen* of modern physics. Now I would suggest that we have retained this discredited concept hermetically, in our notion of genius. Over the next week I want you to look at the photographic iconography of genius. That includes the world of popular culture. I think you might be surprised at the recurrent patterns of expectation and portrayal.'

Lenses and Constellations

'All a lens knows, Owen, is focal length and framing. It can't know anything else. So if I'm to convey that the lens is moving towards knowledge, then it will have to be by one of those means.'

'What about filters?'

'They're just a way of telling the lens that it knows less than it really does.'

John was setting up his camera and tripod so that they pointed to the window of his flat. He had placed a chair immediately before the window. That's where Owen was going to sit.

'A confusion in framing means that the lens doesn't know where to settle, and a confusion of focus means that the lens can't relate to the material it's been presented with. Now if you sit on that chair and speak and I can hear your words clearly, but you are out of focus, then the words are in a definable relation to reality, but not the image. Or a part of the image might be. For example, the roofs over the canal there, they can be in focus, while you're not. What would that tell us?'

'I don't know.'

'Neither do I. Let's find out.'

'You didn't tell me about this. I've not written anything.'

'For once, I'm going to handle you the way you normally handle me. If you're around here disturbing my peace of mind all day, you can earn your keep. Go and sit in the chair and start talking. I'm going to bring you into focus, Mr Treadle.'

So they began, with John working out how to make Owen out of focus, while the world around him came back in. And Owen spoke, haltingly at first, whenever John prompted him. John had made a list of topics, of which Owen knew nothing.

'Tell me about sex, Owen. How much do you remember about that?'

He couldn't be sure whether John was planning on using this as actual footage, or merely experimenting. It was like psychotherapy, with a camera instead of an analyst. The curious thing was how he knew, even as he spoke, that he was out of focus.

'Sometimes walking down the road you'll see not women, but breasts. Breasts and thighs. With women attached. And what is it? A triangle between their legs. A little delta.' For some reason he halted at that word, and explored it. 'Delta. Fur-pelted. A crop of tiny hairs like a miniature forest. This would have been where the armies would come, wouldn't it? The old invasions up the estuary. Nothing softer, no safer homecoming. Cunnus.'

'And your father used to do it with local girls down by the cemetery. Must make you wonder sometimes if you have any half-brothers or sisters walking the streets of Swansea.' John had never played this game before and Owen was not sure he liked it.

'When I was in my teens I met one or two of them. The women, I mean. Some of them not far off my own age. None were attractive. My old man was. A tall slim bloke with thick black hair, a bit like mine, I think. I reckon he picked the ugly ones, knowing they'd be grateful for the attention. I don't think he ever had much trouble pulling. In terms of impregnation, I wouldn't know.'

'Staying with fecundity, you don't have any children of your own, do you?' You son-of-a-bitch, John. Owen faltered, and John with one twist of his finger brought his face into sharp focus for the first time.

'No. Sylvie was pregnant once, as you know, but there was the miscarriage, and . . . things weren't going very well in our marriage at the time and . . . the doctors said it was going to be difficult, maybe very difficult and . . . there'd be a course of treatment whose outcome couldn't be guaranteed and . . . the subject never seems to have come up since. We both got on with our work. People do, you know.'

'When you say that things weren't going very well in your marriage, would that have been because of your various affairs?'

'Possibly.'

'So it could be the case that your wife decided to concentrate on her work, rather than taking the course of treatment, because of her lack of trust in you as a husband and future father.'

'It's possible.' John was finding interesting angles here by sliding in and out of focus. There was a curious dialogue going on between images and words.

'Do you ever think that you might be reproducing the behaviour of your father? Going down to your own cemetery for your own knee-tremblers? Sometimes the cemetery is memory itself, and you have to bury it all down there.' Owen had now fallen silent, and as John brought the lens slowly into focus, the camera registered the tears slowly coursing down his cheeks.

Five-Star Hotels of the Spirit

At any time, day or night, a minimum of five thousand people will be visiting Lady Pneuma's website at the Delta Foundation. That's what her publicity said. They were enquiring about spiritual progress, the falling away of earthly appetites, the movement towards transcendence, the domination of the world by materialist ideology, the one true elemental, which is air, the domicile of light, the home of the angels, Mary's lovely molecules of aquamarine parthenogenesis. Her voice when she spoke on the screen was smooth and syrupy, enough nutrition in it to feed any hungry flock of five thousand. Only ever dressed in white and blue, the colour that contains all colours, and sky colour, vision colour, Mary's colour.

Many of the pilgrims were frank. They could not make what Pneuma called the passage; they could not escape the pain, the gut-writhing pain that resulted from their withdrawal from the dark matter of food. It was as though the wretched substance had too great a hold on their spirits. Was it possible that some might be unworthy? None were unworthy, replied the transcendent Lady, none. All could make the passage, but not all would find it easy, and not all could do it at once. She herself had not found it easy. The golden flesh her body now boasted had once been white, anorexic, withdrawn. The light had only started shining through it from the inside once she had made the passage, the first one of the modern age.

The world was snares; it was a locked sepulchre of snakes

and trumpets. No one should feel unable to follow her, but it might take time. For those still encountering problems, there was a new DVD, available from nowhere except the Delta Fellowship. Its price of £30 was not unreasonable, given the love and dedication which had gone into its making. The first edition had sold out completely.

*

By the time the two shepherds found her, Alex Gregory had passed the point of recovery. She was now so enfeebled that her organs had largely ceased functioning. The men could not believe the sight before them, the little bundle of bones and parched skin she had become. They could not understand what had brought her so low. One of them had a mobile. He phoned the emergency services. A helicopter arrived within half an hour, but the paramedics' attempts to re-hydrate her and put some glucose into her body by means of a drip were to no avail. She died twenty-four hours later in hospital. By then her father and mother were at her side. She never re-gained consciousness, and so was unable to answer the urgent questions her father wanted to put to her.

A week later he was given the book and the DVD, *The One True Elemental* and *Lady Pneuma Speaks*. The following day, in an attempt to combat his grief with activity, he started reading and watching. He started making notes.

'Is this why you starved yourself to death, my darling?' he asked. Mr Patrick Gregory, one-time policeman and now the owner of Lex Security, decided to discover the precise factors which had led to his daughter's death. He would look upon Lady Pneuma and the Delta Foundation with the same dispassionate, forensic eye with which he'd focused on so much else in his life. But he couldn't pretend there wasn't a sharp, personal edge to this particular inquiry. Someone was going to pay.

Three weeks later, he had read every word Lady Pneuma had ever written (or at least every one still available) and seen all the performances on video and DVD. He had used some old contacts in the Metropolitan Police to check out a few things for him, and had been given a contact in the Inland Revenue (presently conducting their own investigation) who had proved particularly useful. He didn't know Detective Inspector Gregory (retired), nor had he heard of Lex Security, but he had been told about the death of the man's daughter by their mutual contact. And he felt no obligation whatsoever to protect Lady Pneuma, *aka* Rachel Askarli, from anyone or anything. Why should he?

And so Patrick Gregory became Detective Inspector once more. He studied his materials. Included among which, one of the few other things in that bothie apart from Alex's ever-shrinking body, was her diary from the last six months of her life. After reading this through twice, he realised that there was one other person he wanted to confront, apart from the female apostle of inanition. There was also a man he wanted to see and talk to. A man who lived in Chester.

Confessional

When Owen walked into the room, he saw John adjusting the camera on its tripod. The chair was already in place. The light was coming through the window. Owen wished he were somewhere else, anywhere else.

'Ready, Owen? If you want to sit down we can start.' So Owen sat and they started.

'Most people live inside their memory the way they live in a country or a family. But you leave yours periodically, the same way an emigré leaves a country or a home-breaker leaves his wife and kids. Have you ever thought about that?'

'No.'

'Have you ever wondered if your anterograde amnesia is a form of escape? It has happened a number of times in your life now, hasn't it?'

'Yes it has, and no I haven't.'

'You never forget words, do you Owen? You have more words at your disposal than any other human being I've ever met, but the words seem to get disconnected from their referents sometimes. Do you think this might have something to do with the way you privilege the words over the realities they're meant to disclose?'

'What do you mean?'

'I seem to be doing a lot of talking here, when you're the one who's meant to be coming back into focus. I'm just the lensman. I mean that if a man is sufficiently taken with his own use of words, sufficiently immersed in his own rhetoric, then he runs the danger of finding his own words more real than the reality they might express. Perhaps they become the only reality he recognises. That would amount to a psychosis. Or do you believe that the artist has the right to re-create reality?'

'It's not a right, it's a duty. What do you think Picasso did?'

'Well, in those minotaur images we looked at in *Down In The Cave*, I would have said that what makes them so moving is precisely their relationship to reality. The relationship between the minotaur and the artist is evident.'

'The minotaur is both the victim and the victimiser. He both kills and is killed. Enter the labyrinth and you're a marked man.'

'Or woman. But then Picasso was telling a kind of truth, surely. We see in the minotaur's eyes, in the desperation of his desire, a kind of hopelessness in the man too. Isn't this a kind of truthfulness, which is one way of talking about the obligations of memory? Isn't the word truthfulness a way of saying that the obligations of memory are inescapable, in art or out of it?'

'Picasso also said he could look directly at the sun. He was the only man who'd ever lived who could stare at the sun without having his sockets scorched. Am I in focus at the moment, John?'

'No.'

'How out of focus am I?'

'Not sure there's an effective terminology for degrees of unfocus.'

'Is the world behind me in focus? The canals; the rooftops; the old mill?'

'Yes.'

'Well, I suppose if a man can't be in focus, at least his world can be.'

'And his memory, Owen? Can he leave that in a warehouse, I wonder?'

John twisted the lens and Owen was in sharp focus for the first time during the whole of that shoot.

'A warehouse. Memory in a warehouse. Was that where they were screaming then?'

'Only one of them was screaming, Owen. Don't you remember? You wrote the scene and insisted on playing it out that way. I could easily have made do with a few emblematic shots and some montage, but no, you had to have the screams and the scene *in situ*. You only hit her with the whole thing ten minutes before we had to do it. You only hit me with the whole thing at the same time. Don't you remember? I think you do remember, Owen. You can't do such things in life and then discard them by cutting the memories loose. I don't think that's truthful. And you always insisted it was the truth we were after.'

There was silence for a few moments and Owen's face became concentrated in the way that it did when he was really working. John kept the image in focus. We can go back out again later. But this was the image of the return of memory, and he wanted it sharp. He had assumed that the moment of memory's return would be redemptive; now he realised it might be tragic. Make for a better film.

'It was my hand, wasn't it, gripping her, keeping her in place, though the camera couldn't see that, could it, John? We'd set the shot up so that I could be invisible, holding her in place. You used the hand-held camera, so the confusion was part of what we were filming. She trusted me so much. "You'll be there, won't you, Owen?" She kept saying that, and I kept saying, "Yes Alex, everything is going to be fine." The softness: that's where they want their hardness to be. It's the delta where everything goes in, and I suppose everything comes out finally. So many shouts. They were Romans, weren't they, and Serbians, Soviet soldiers in

1945 entering Berlin, Japanese conscripts in Manchuria with their comfort women. Their uniforms didn't matter. We had those anonymous baggy suits made for them with camouflage markings. A warehouse with a concrete floor. Could have been a basilica, a transit hut, any house of detention in any town, at any time. That was the point wasn't it, to show the way history kept repeating itself. She didn't have any shoes on, did she, Johnny? It must have been cold for her, you know. Those hard men moving in. Heading for the triangle, the delta. They were going to get into that, even though the woman the triangle led into wanted to keep them out so badly. And her cries were real now, weren't they? This would be superb, wouldn't it, John, when we saw the footage afterwards? The awards would roll in for this one. A genuine passion play of our time.' Owen was smiling now, an oddly detached, entirely uncheering smile.

Very slowly, John Tamworth slid the camera out of focus, and let the video continue running, with a shadowy blur in front of it, now fallen silent.

The following morning, Owen tried to look at himself in the mirror, but he couldn't find anything there. Alex had told him some story, he remembered, about how it was a Taoist doctrine that evil couldn't look at itself in the mirror. The silent shriek of recognition abolished the looker. But it wasn't that. Each time he looked in the mirror his own face kept being replaced by that of Alex Gregory. He could even hear the gentle fluting of her voice as she said to him, 'Oh come on, Owen, you wouldn't really ask me to do that.' He had asked her though; more than asked her, hadn't he? Even held her in place while the images were made.

As he stood looking in the mirror, John Tamworth was knocking on the door of Sylvie's house.

'I need the coat. The greatcoat you told me about.'

They sat together in the kitchen drinking coffee.

'It feels bad, John.'

'It is bad, Sylvie. Somebody died this time. Owen wants to make a film about memory. Maybe he wants to turn his life into a film, the way we turned Alex Gregory's death into one. First we filmed it, then she lived it. Died it. I don't know. I want the greatcoat. The one he always wears when he switches off the lights inside and goes walkabout.'

'What are you going to do to him, John?'

'Make him real.'

'By turning him into film?'

'That's how he made Alex real. Altogether too real.'

'What's happening with *Deva*?'

'Don't know. Not going to be easy, is it? Have you seen it yet?' She shook her head.

'Should I?'

'Don't ask me. It's very powerful. Too powerful maybe. Images should keep their distance. Don't expect to be eating popcorn. You'd choke on it. Where's the coat?'

'Down in the cellar.'

So they went down together. He folded it over his arm. The tabloid newspaper was still sticking out of its pocket.

Deva. *Deva Victrix*. A Roman goddess of war. She urged her troops on to slaughter. Chester, the city of the eagles, had been named after her, and the river still carried her name. The Severn was Sabrina. The Romans couldn't be in a place for a week before they populated the landscape with their gods. Gods in the sky, gods in the earth, goddesses in the trees, nymphs flitting back and forth, trying to escape the impregnating force of the big powers, never succeeding except by taking a different form entirely, taking on a different life. Metamorphoses. Vibrant constellations. Picasso was at home with this. He was the Ovid of the visual arts. The world of the

Vollard Suite is a world of Mediterranean classicism. Ancient sculptors lay back with a glass of wine and a Roman beauty. Nakedness is a form of aristocratic languor. But breaking in to the world of plinths and memories and draperies and afternoon divans awaiting their sumptuous nudes, the minotaur arrives. So what's his place in this landscape then?

Not at home, that's for sure. Is any labyrinth a home? He is an asylum-seeker in the halls of a chilly culture, a vagrant appetite that can't be accommodated inside any museum. He is a hunter hunted. His animality cannot be denied, but neither can his intelligence. He is an animal who understands that what intelligence he has dooms him to extinction, but sadly for him he can't escape his own intelligence. Not only must he die, but he must watch his own dying. Sometimes he seems to be more of a man than the other men around him. But those horns of his will dig in to the flesh of others. The appetites cannot be put for ever out of focus, however intelligent the minotaur's eyes might be. His intelligence is at least in part an acknowledgment that he can't disown his own desire.

Picasso had been to the *corrida* thousands of times. He had seen how the bull's horns heave away at the picadors' horses, thrusting, goring, penetrating, even while the spears slice in to his bloody back. He cannot cease from this; this is what he does. Stopping is not an option. This tragic pressure was what held and fascinated Picasso. He simply couldn't leave the subject alone.

In some of the engravings and etchings, the creature wasn't far-off urbane, drinking his wine, caressing his sweetheart. In others the pressure of his physicality was urgent and baffling. In pressing against the body of the woman, he was pressing against his own body too, while youths with wreathed foreheads played their flutes. In one, astonishingly – what an artist Picasso was – the woman sat and watched him in his sleep, a curly tangle of unfathomability, veiled by a curtain. In another he was crouched on top of her, his bull-belly drumming away at the delta where his fluids might finally flow. In some of them he was the bull crouching in submission to his own final sword, except that there was no sword. There was a human presence, which was enough to quell him. Perhaps Theseus hadn't wielded his magic sword at all, merely spoken. The words themselves had made him realise that his miserable kingdom was at an end. And that was the other thing about the minotaur's death: it was so clearly desired. Not resisted but accepted. And the women looked on. Rows upon rows of women's faces looked on as the minotaur lay dying, his bellow now an aria. He had become beautiful at last.

Henry's favourite was the drypoint of 1933, *Minotaur Kneeling Over Sleeping Girl*. He was entranced. There was no hint of violence, present or to come. It was only too evident that this was an act of adoration. If she had spoken in her sleep and demanded it, he would have accepted self-annihilation as his fate.

The bell rang and Henry rose from his reverie. In the gallery, smiling and be-ribboned, stood Marie Coleforth, owner of the Heights Gallery.

'Hello Henry. I've brought you a present. Two presents, actually.' From the Marks and Spencer bag she produced a bottle of chianti, and the vegetarian pizza which he had made for Miriam French. 'There's only one catch: I'm hungry and I wouldn't mind a glass of wine.'

So they sat in the Picasso Room and ate and drank.

'I'm beginning to think my beloved Pablo must have been Italian.'

'How's that?'

'The amount of pizza and chianti that's consumed in here.'

'I'll bring you paella next time. But looking at these pictures, I suppose we could check if there's a Spanish speciality involving bull's testicles.'

'I'm sure there must be, but I'd rather not find out. I've grown too fond of my minotaur friend in here to want to eat his balls.'

'Why are you fond of him?' He had only dealt with Marie on business matters before; it intrigued him how coquettish she seemed to have become suddenly. He wondered, was she normally like that with all men, or was it especially for him? Look at the way she's dressed. But then it couldn't be especially for him; they'd both been around far too long for that. She was certainly taller than Henry, though the hair she'd had spiked added a few more inches. And she wore heels too, so it was possible that in her stocking feet they'd come out evens. Brown eyes warm with amusement. Why are you so fond of the minotaur, Henry? The lady asked you a question.

'I wondered if we might have shared an address for a while inside the labyrinth.'

'You've prepared this really nicely, Henry.'

'I switched the oven on, yes. Odd how women always compliment you for heating things up. It's like being given a certificate for finding your way to the bathroom. What do you think? That the Meals on Wheels lady normally does my dinner? You must have a look at my shirts later. The way I wash and iron them, you'll probably have me crowned King of Hungary.' Marie carried on smiling. For a woman who'd just been ditched by her husband of fifteen years, she looked remarkably cheerful about things. Maybe it is my presence, he thought. Women did seem to smile at him a lot. Minotaurs and women: they both trusted him.

'Miriam really enjoyed her evening here, you know.'

'Evidently. She went back and made you write down my

secret recipe for buying pizzas. Thank God I didn't do the minotaur's testicles with rice '

'Said you were better company than any man she could remember for a long time.'

'Did she really say that?'

'You were very articulate on the subject of Picasso, she said, but then I could have told her that. She found it such a relief from the butch prattlers in London these days talking about their cars or football or property prices.' Here Marie winked. Henry, you are being winked at. What's going on here? 'She said if she'd not been gay, she'd have given you one.'

'I could have dressed up as a woman for the night; I'm very adaptable.'

'You don't have to dress up as a woman for me, Henry.'

The Fade on the Greatcoat

When Owen walked into the room and saw the camera on its tripod, with John hovering over it, and then the chair with the greatcoat draped over it, he almost turned and walked out again.

'Nearly ready, Owen.' John Tamworth had become aware that in taking Owen in and out of focus he was sliding him in and out of existence. He didn't pretend to himself that there wasn't a certain amount of pleasure here. Owen had some-times made his life seriously unpleasant. The affairs, the un-predictability, the recurrent amnesia, the insouciant come-as-you-may lordliness; all this had grated with John, an old-style socialist who believed that human beings should try to sink their egos into the greater community. He had always believed that, and he still believed it. No amount of talk about markets and freedom would stop him believing it. At some impenetr-able level, he suspected that Owen believed it too, but it didn't affect his behaviour much. Owen had managed to layer John with resentments over the years, and it was only now for the first time that they were all being given the chance of a decent airing. Owen made his way over to the chair and sat down.

'Put the greatcoat on.'

'I'm not cold.'

'The temperature has nothing to do with it. We're making a film, remember? Alex was cold, very cold, but that didn't stop us filming, did it? Put the greatcoat on, Owen.' And Owen did as he was told. John was feeling more authoritative with every take. 'What do you do when you have the greatcoat on?'

'I go to see Alfred.'

'And what happens with Alfred?'

'Alfred always wants to find out what's in my mind.'

'Why?'

'Ask Alfred.'

'He's not here.'

'He's not far from here. Ask me questions I can answer.'

'Does Alfred have his own images to live in too?'

'Yes. Most of them come from the Book of Revelation. For Alfred the world is filled with beasts and redeemers, with angels of light and servants of Babylon, whoring after strange gods, and fornicating in the temple. Every inch of reality is contested by the forces of good and the forces of evil. He lives in the scriptural equivalent of a Fellini film.'

'Why did you make us do that rape scene at the last minute, Owen?'

'I'd been trying to think about it from the other way around. Abu Ghraib, Lindy England, giving her victory sign over a pile of male bodies. History usually arranged it otherwise. But that's progress for you. And a digital image too, instantly transmittable. What a difference democracy makes. Even women can sexually taunt the enemy, given sufficient military resources behind them. I was trying to work out how we form those images we recognised when we see ourselves coming the other way, out of mirrors, out of photographs.'

'The costumes were anonymous, John, in case you've forgotten, because the plot was transposable. Chester, Bosnia, Rome, Iraq. We didn't spend too long in Iraq after that contractor was kidnapped though, did we? Decided most of our necessary effects could probably be achieved back home in the studio after all. So the studio was the world then, John. It was the Globe and the globe. That's what we decided. The passion happened anywhere and everywhere. One warehouse with a concrete floor was reality, and I was trying to make it real. Wasn't that our job?

'What does military occupation mean except that order is to be brought from disorder, and that can only mean that the agents of disorder are the native inhabitants. Some force will need to be applied to get them to see sense. The sense of the *imperium*. Force has a tendency to generate more of itself, and appetites are universal. So bodies get used for what they normally get used for in war: the accommodation of someone else's need, or a lot of people's needs – a lot of soldiers' needs. A certain amount of humiliation might as well be thrown in, just to show that no apologies are required when you have the power. Men have always humiliated women and boasted about it. I was trying to convey that, not glorify it.'

John remembered reading once how, during the recording of *In A Silent Way*, Miles Davis had told the guitarist John McLaughlin: 'Play the guitar as though you don't know how to play the guitar.' That was what John was learning to do with his camera. He focused finally not on Owen's face, but on the greying greatcoat. Then he pressed the fade button.

Back at the Signum

Sylvie had switched on the overhead projector and slid the image into place on the glass.

'What are we looking at. Any guesses? Lionel?' Lionel looked at the image on the screen for a moment.

'Microbes?'

'That's a very good guess, Lionel. It's totally wrong, but it's a very good guess. And the reason it's a good guess is that you realised you are looking through a lens. The image is circular. There are little blooms in it, little pink squirms among the green. Little blobs of something. Microbes, molecules, viruses. Actually they're little blobs of light. This is a picture from the Hubble Telescope, and what we're seeing is the Large Magellanic Cloud. It's 160,000 light years away. The light left home to travel in our direction not during the time of the last Ice Age, but the one before that. This light has been doing some serious travelling, before we made this image out of it. Because we did have to make the image; this isn't just a snapshot in space. This image has been constructed. And there are times with the Hubble images when aesthetics seems to play as large a part as scientific enquiry. We have that on Dr Helsey's authority.' Fucking Tom.

'Lionel thought he was looking through a microscope, but in fact he was looking through a telescope. You have to be aware of both the lenses and the constellations they're pointing at, otherwise you can't make sense of reality. Now, I've spoken to you before about the seventeenth century. Let's remember Swift.

Here's that passage from *Gulliver's Travels* I've already read to you. This is Brobdingnag:

The Kingdom is much pestered with Flies in Summer; and these odious Insects, each of them as big as a *Dunstable Lark*, hardly gave me any Rest while I sat at Dinner, with their continual Humming and Buzzing about mine Ears. They would sometimes alight upon my Victuals, and leave their loathsome Excrement or Spawn behind, which to me was very visible, although not to the Natives of that Country, whose large Opticks were not so acute as mine in viewing smaller Objects.

'This passage simply could not have been written without the publication of *Micrographia*, with its illustrations of the large grey drone-fly and the flea. We can actually point to a publication and announce that this one book has changed the way we see reality. We're looking at existence through different lenses. And what's interesting about the passage from Swift is his awareness of different optical realms; our optics are appropriate to our functions, and in a sense both the telescope and the microscope have started to confuse the issue, to the evident distress of Pope. Remember what he wrote:

Why has not man a miscroscopic eye?
For this plain reason: man is not a fly.

'The fact is that Gulliver's eye in Brobdingnag is a microscope, and much pain it causes him as he gazes on human lice upon the human body. The most famous of the illustrations in *Micrographia* had been a sixteen-inch fold-out of a louse. The genius of *Gulliver's Travels* was to understand that perception had been altered for ever by the introduction of both the telescope and the microscope.

'And the vast space of the Baroque entered had entered Milton's mind through a telescope, though by the time he came to portray that vastness, he was himself already blind. He'd had a look through one though; remember he describes his visit to Galileo in *Areopagitica*. Though the words of *Paradise Lost* were written by a blind man, they seem to see the vast spaces more vividly than even the most apocalyptic of its illustrators, John Martin. And what they see is the demolition of boundaries. The reality had been so powerfully lensed that its reality didn't fade, even in blindness.

'What does all this teach us? That we live with lenses, we live before lenses and we live behind them. We can't imagine what life would be like without them.'

As Sylvie walked down the corridor she saw Alison coming the other way, a large smile on her face.

'Next week. Wednesday at 11 o'clock in 1101. If we all vote together, we can get him out.'

This was the long-expected vote of no confidence which, if carried, would go all the way to Senate, and result either in Hamish's dismissal or diplomatic re-deployment. No sooner had she stepped into her room than the phone rang. It was Hamish.

'I was wondering if we might have a little chat at some point. Some point in the very near future, I mean.'

Inquisitorial Lens

Owen looked again at the chair with the greatcoat draped over it, and John adjusting his lens. He felt sick.

'Could we skip one day, John?'

'No. I said if you wanted to stay here, you'd have to let me work. This is my work at the moment, and you're a part of it. Anyway, you're going to have to do this sooner or later, and you might as well do it with me. Remember, I don't charge. Regard it as a form of therapy. Put the coat on, Owen.'

John noticed that Owen no longer met his gaze while the camera was running. Nor did he look into the lens. He simply stared before him. The continuing interrogation had induced a kind of autism in his physiognomy. But John was going to produce an expression from his old friend today. Just see if he didn't.

'When you write, are you trying to describe reality or re-create it?'

'I don't think those things are incompatible.'

'But in *Loving Every Minute*, the woman was not an actual woman, was she? This woman, a victim of violence who had ended up conniving in her own entrapment, she came out of your head.'

'But I could only put her together from observation. I didn't make her out of nothing. I made her out of something.'

'In *Down in the Cave*, it was simpler, I think. You were making connections. Connections between the paintings on the walls of the caves and Picasso's images of bulls and minotaurs. *Corridas* and labyrinths. The mazes at Knossos and the riddling way that art and ritual complicate things to finally make them simpler, to take us through a necessary passage of darkness back out to the light.'

'That was simpler, yes.'

'But in *Deva*, you took the facts of war as you saw them, and you collated them. You shaped a universal template of the reality of war, a template which had never existed in any actual war.'

'War is a moveable feast.'

'Or a moveable sacrifice. And then you tested that reality against a number of characters who were fictional. The bereaved old lady, the ruined man, the brutal commander and the girl . . . what was her name, Owen?'

'You know what her name was.'

'But I want you to tell me.' For the first time he said it. That name. Very slowly.

'Alex. Alex Gregory.'

'And you did something I've seen you do before. To help you find the reality you were searching for, you used her mind. You explored fictional realities through an actual mind and body.'

'It's not unknown.'

'Maybe not. But I've never known anyone else do it to the same extent. To find out how she'd act on a bed, you fucked her first. That shows great commitment to your work, Owen. Your pursuit of the perfect image involved her becoming one.' Owen had now put his head in his hands; John let the lens come slowly into focus.

'And to see how she would react to being raped you set the scene up so that she almost was. With the local louts who'd been drinking, and weren't really acting much at all. If the rest of us hadn't been there, then they would have raped her, wouldn't they?'

'Bresson didn't like using professional actors. He preferred people from the shops and the street.'

'You must have known how it would cut into her mind, Owen. You'd been having an affair with her for a year. Everyone could see she was vulnerable, but you'd got to see her at much closer quarters than the rest of us. Why couldn't you trust me to fake it?' Owen's face now swung up out of his hands.

'Because I wanted it real. I didn't want it faked. I wanted the actual terror in her eyes. That's what we're trying to do, isn't it? Convey some reality in a world so filled with images that no one bothers to look at them any more.'

'Well, you succeeded, all right. Take the newspaper out of your greatcoat pocket.'

'I don't want to.'

'And Alex didn't want those boys tearing away her clothes and sticking their hands up her thighs while you held her hand and told her to stay there. You must remember the things we do in search of our truthful image, Owen. Take the newspaper out and turn to the middle pages.'

There was a photograph of Alex, a picture from the family album, with her smiling, her full cheeks bright with sun and nourishment. And then there was a photograph of the bothie on the headland, the bleak sea beyond, and the headline: *Why Did This Girl Starve To Death Alone?* For the first time in all the hours of footage, John started to zoom very slowly towards Owen's face. Which had frozen. No tears. No expression. Nothing. He held the shot for a full minute before switching the camera off.

Inside the Labyrinth

In the year 2001 Michael Landy took all the possessions he had acquired in his thirty-eight years of life and had them publicly destroyed in what had once been the C&A store in London's Oxford Street. The items circled around slowly on metal conveyors until finally being cut up or dismantled and fed into shredding machines. Nothing was exempt, neither Landy's birth-certificate nor his beloved Saab, not even his recordings of David Bowie. If it belonged to Landy then it had to be destroyed. As installation art-works go *Breakdown* was amongst the purest. You could only watch as the commodities moved slowly towards their extinction inside a mausoleum of commodities. All the images were destroyed. Except that an image had preserved their destruction. Even images of self-destruction left their traces in images, one of which Sylvie was looking at now. It hung on her wall, commemorating the moment when everything it represented disappeared. There was a tap on the door. It was Hamish.

'I was wondering if we might have that little word. Would you mind? Perhaps we could go over to my office. I have some things there I might need to refer to.'

And so Hamish walked back to his office, and Sylvie followed him a moment later.

'Do sit down, Sylvie. Make yourself comfortable.' She looked at the small face, grown tight over the years with unrelenting calculation.

'You may be aware that next Wednesday there will be an

extraordinary meeting downstairs. The meeting has been called by one or two disgruntled members of staff, who have taken against me for a gallimaufry of reasons. They plan to pass a vote of no-confidence. To do that requires, according to our rather eccentric constitution, that seven people support the motion. That would have to include you, according to my reckoning. I just wanted to make sure I could count on your support.'

'You'll have to wait until the meeting. I haven't heard the arguments yet.'

'No, but you understand the principles, surely. There have been some absurd allegations flying around that I listen in on people's calls, examine their emails, or snoop on their communications, as one complainant put it. What I actually do, of course, is monitor communications of various sorts.

'To make sure nothing amiss is happening, or is likely to. There's been a resurgence of racism, even in academic life, and I have no intention of letting any of that happen here.'

'I can't give you any assurances, Hamish.'

'That's a shame, because another matter has come up, which I had hoped could be shelved indefinitely, but it's possible, I suppose, that it can't.' He then pulled open the drawer of his desk and took out a sheet of paper. She could see the university letterhead. 'I have here a complaint, of rather grave nature, concerning your behaviour. It comes from Dr Thomas Helsey who, in fact, in a matter of a couple of months, will be Professor Helsey.

'Tell me, Sylvie, do you really think it in order for you to use your special privileges here to seduce a married member of staff, after you have invited him to contribute to one of your lecture courses?'

'I didn't seduce him.'

'Well, that's not what Dr Helsey says. His allegation is quite specific. A friendly meeting to discuss his part in your lecture course, an invitation to return here so you could lend him a book you thought would interest him. Then, before he'd had much of a chance to consider the matter, since I believe you had both been drinking heavily, events took place which he can now only recollect with shame. He has made a full confession to his wife, apparently, and has explained himself fully to me. He apologised for showing such disrespect to this institution, as to treat it as little more than a brothel, and I have accepted his apology as given in good faith.

'But as for you, Sylvie, I honestly don't know what to say. I have your husband phoning up here, desperate to find out where you've been all night. At the same time another gentleman, certainly not your husband, phoning through the switchboard to leave coded love-messages, and then within days, hours for all I know, you are using the rooms in this institution to seduce senior members of the academic staff. Married ones too. If all this surfaces, I really can't see how your position here would continue to be tenable for long.'

Sylvie stared at that face she'd never much liked, and liked even less now that it was imprinted with its smile of victory.

'I hope we understand one another. I shall put this letter from Dr Helsey away, and sincerely hope I don't have to make it public. I am still jealous of this place's reputation, even if others aren't. Now perhaps you'd like to go, since I have some important work to get on with.'

Special Dispensation

Ex-Detective-Inspector Patrick Gregory had always been a methodical man, and he was now collating his evidence. The contact at the Inland Revenue had phoned him that morning.

'She's at the Claymore. Top floor. Been there six or seven weeks. Booked in under the name of Smith. Now there's imagination for you. Beverley Smith.'

He had kept his Detective-Inspector's ID, though it was long out of date, even though employing it as he was about to, would have landed him in serious trouble, were it ever to come to light. He had done this a few times before, and had no intention of being any less competent in his deception this time.

'Any chance of a room on the top floor?' he asked the receptionist over the phone. 'I have happy memories of a delightful weekend there with my wife many years ago. Being a widower now, I like to revive these memories from time to time.' Inspector Gregory was granted his wish. He would have to move quickly, for he would soon be spending serious money staying at the Claymore.

'You're a widower now, are you?' his wife asked him from the kitchen.

'Thankfully not.'

So it was that a neat, middle-aged man in a suit and tie, his shoes polished and his cases trim and tidy, arrived at the Claymore Hotel for three nights. He had chosen a dark suit. That way, should he choose, he could be one of the hotel officials. As the porter carried his case in to the room, Patrick gave him a substantially larger tip than he normally would.

'Thank you very much, sir,' the porter said. 'Anything else I can do for you?'

'Yes, there is one thing. An old friend of mine, Beverley Smith, has been staying here. Been here a few weeks now. Do you know which room she'd be in?' The porter pointed.

'Down the bottom of the corridor. On this side. Keeps herself very much to herself.'

'Good old Beverley. Hasn't changed much then. See if I can coax her out of herself for an evening.'

Patrick put away his things and rang room service. He asked for two gin and tonics. When they arrived ten minutes later, he waited until the waiter had disappeared back in to the lift, then he held the tray aloft and made his way down to the bottom of the corridor.

'Room service, madame,' he said as he knocked. The voice sounded clearly from within.

'What?' Patrick simply turned the handle and walked in.

The room was not like his room. It had been draped with muslin sheets. They were everywhere, even across the window. And the woman lay on a sofa, dressed in white and blue. Her face was bronzed, and her body that of a well-fed woman, not plump exactly, but edging in that direction. Her feet were bare and he could see that they had been manicured and the toenails painted. He had a distinct feeling she had not done this herself. And there was a plate beside her, empty.

'You ordered two gin and tonics, Madame.'

'I did not.' Her voice was deep and authoritative. She was used to wielding power, he could see that. 'You're not the usual one, either. I told them only to send me Charlie. Please remind them of my instructions, and take the drinks away. I don't drink, as a matter of fact.'

As he turned to go he caught sight of the book. He knew it well enough. He had now read his daughter's copy three times, making notes. He closed the door behind him, went down the corridor and re-entered his own room. He sat down on the chair by the window and started to drink one of the gin and tonics.

'Alex, if you'd only listened to me on the subject of logic and evidence, you'd still be here, my love.'

From the age of fifteen, she had exasperated him, though the exasperation never cancelled his devotion to his only child. Mystical minerals, astrology, Kabbalah; whatever represented the most radical deviation from the traditions of western science, then that must evidently be where mental health and well-being lay. He could never read more than a few pages of whatever gibberish she'd taken to lately without a small explosion.

'But Alex, the tradition of thought we've inherited is probably the richest the world has ever seen, whatever its shortcomings. Don't throw it all away for this . . . this prattle.'

Her father the policeman, you see, committed to his archaic notions of deduction and forensic proof. Which he was about to employ again right now. For ex-Detective-Inspector Gregory was indeed a rigorously logical men. Even his colleagues in the force used to remark upon it. He opened his brief-case and took out his pad. He wrote the number *One* at the top of the sheet and beside that he wrote *Sun Tan*. This woman who never leaves her suite looks as though she has spent the last month on a Mediterranean beach. He took the hotel brochure from the table and flipped through it. The solarium was in the basement.

He took the lift down. He walked through the entrance. The woman in the white coat looked up from her magazine.

'Do you have an appointment, sir?'

'No, there's been an emergency and I must find Miss Beverley Smith. Is she here at the moment?' The woman clicked her screen and scanned.

'No, she already had her session earlier.'

'Thank you.' First problem solved then, without any need for the inner light. He went back up to his room, and wrote the number *Two* on the page. At the side of this he wrote the word *Food*. There were a number of possibilities. Either she used room service or she went out herself and brought things back, or she ate out. He couldn't quite see Lady Pneuma coming back with sandwiches in their plastic wrappings. The way she had lain on that sofa made budget indoor picnics seem unlikely. If it was room-service, then it had to be someone she trusted, and if she went out, then how did she make sure no one could recognise her? His contact in the Inland Revenue had told him that she greatly valued her privacy.

'I mean she lives on air, Mr Gregory, so she obviously likes hiding in clouds.'

Patrick found the kitchen. There was much coming and going. He stopped one of the cooks.

'Charlie about?' The man in the white hat nodded over to a tall, thin young man, fairly good-looking in a facially-blemished, adolescent way.

'Charlie, could I have a word?' Charlie immediately looked hunted. Patrick knew that look. He had encountered it thousands of times. 'I just want to ask you a few questions.' They went out to the corridor. Charlie's forehead was damp from the heat.

'I haven't done anything wrong.'

'I never said you had.' Patrick pulled his old ID out of his pocket, all the same. Charlie took one look at it and seemed to sweat a little more.

'Do you do the deliveries for Miss Beverley Smith?' Charlie now started to look very nervous indeed, and Patrick decided this was the moment to use his non-existent position as an officer of the law.

'Look, son, this needn't go any further than you and me if you tell me what I need to know. I won't tell your boss.'

'She said it would be all right?'

'What would be all right?'

'What we did up there. I told her I'd get the sack if anyone found out about it.'

What they did up there. He hadn't even thought of that, what with Lady Pneuma being so free from cravings of the flesh.

'Do you take her food up?'

'When she has it up there. She usually goes out each day.'

'What time?'

'Between five and six. Different places, I think.'

'Right, now you go back to work and say nothing to anyone, you understand? Got a mobile, have you, in case I need to contact you?' Charlie gave him the number. 'I'll be in touch.'

At 4.50 Patrick sat in the lobby and watched. He was a good, anonymous watcher, but his watching turned up nothing. All variety of life passed through, Africans, Chinese, the odd Muslim woman in full garb, but there was no Lady Pneuma. At 6.10 he went back up to the top floor and knocked on her door. He knocked louder and louder, but there was no reply. He went down to the solarium, the restaurant, the bar. Nothing. Obviously she'd vanished into thin air, another trick she'd learnt.

This happened on the second day too, until a thought struck Patrick. He had been working his way through possibilities and discounting them one by one. But his eye had been caught by a particular shape. He had seen it come and go. He smiled to himself, nodded his head, went back up to his room, and phoned the number marked laundry.

'Beverley Smith asked me to phone down. Is her burqa ready?'

'That's the long black number, is it?'

'That's the one, yes.'

'One of them is. The other one only came in last night.'

'That's fine. If you could leave it on her door.'

'There's a note not to do that. To either deliver by hand or return.'

'From now on, it will be all right on the door. She feels the time has come to make a public statement about her beliefs as a Muslim. Thank you.'

So it was that on the third evening, Patrick Gregory followed Lady Pneuma, to the small restaurant along Piccadilly, where he watched her eat soup and bread roll, steak and chips, apple pie and ice cream, all washed down with a glass of wine, and a coffee to follow. Having carefully positioned himself two tables down, and set up his trusty old camera, he managed to take at least ten shots of her. She had removed enough of her face-covering, thinking herself safe in the corner, and was entirely oblivious to everyone around her as she ate. He could not remember ever seeing anyone eat with more concentration. At the next table a man and a woman were in dispute.

'I don't just want sex, Jack. I want love. You just want sex, don't you?'

'Ideally.'

'Sex without love. Or responsibility.'

'Whenever possible.'

*

It was a special dispensation. She had overcome the urges of the flesh, any carnal longings, so completely that she was now at liberty to indulge them if she chose. Because this would have been so hard to explain to her disciples, she chose to keep all this to herself. She could live without food, drink or sex, and yet she felt it made it easier for her to relate to her growing flock, and their all-too-human appetites, to remind herself continually what those appetites were, how they blocked the light, how they could swallow the air and turn it into dark matter again. For days at a time, she might not eat, since it had long ago ceased to be a requirement, but then at other times she re-joined them – out of choice; out of, if the truth were known, a kind of love and mercy.

For she was not cruel. Even Charlie would end up more spiritual than he began, for she gave him a little instruction as they went. In any case, she gave him money. Money. They'd have to be making another DVD soon.

By the time Rachel Askarli had paid her bill, resumed her facial protection and stood up to leave, Patrick Gregory had all the images he needed. He'd nailed her. He put a twenty-pound note in the bemused waiter's hand and followed her out. He was tempted to step up alongside and introduce himself, but he mustn't put pleasure before business. He might frighten her off. He had one aim, and one only: to expose her for the charlatan she was and make sure nobody else ever suffered the fate of his daughter. When he got back to the hotel he phoned Charlie's mobile.

'Is she expecting you up there tonight?'

'Ten o'clock. That's when my shift ends.'

'Get herself dolled up for these little trysts, does she?'

'I'll say. Suspenders, stockings, the lot. She could make quite a bit of money over in Soho.'

'Well, you forget it tonight, son, but don't tell her you won't be there. I'm arranging a little surprise for her, and after that you won't see her again anyway. Just count yourself lucky you still have a job, and keep your mouth shut.'

So it was that evening, when Lady Pneuma, *aka* Rachel Askarli, heard the knock on the door and heard the name Charlie, she called 'Come in,' and found herself being photographed in a state of contrived *déshabillé*. With a glass in her hand. The stockings attached to her suspender belt were deep blue, Mary's colour. Charlie had liked those. The newspaper was very grateful to Patrick Gregory, and he had made sure they paid him more than enough to recompense him for his stay at the hotel. It was in fact a newspaper he never read, detesting its shallow vulgarity and its relentless appetite for destroying reputations. That was exactly why he had chosen it. That's why its photographer was here tonight.

Quorate

'So all we need to do now is vote. Would all those who wish to vote for the motion of no-confidence in the present Director of Studies please raise your hand. Hands went up one by one around the table. Hamish's supporters kept theirs firmly on the mahogany before them. And Alison was counting. There was only one hand still needed to set the proceedings in motion. Sylvie hadn't wanted to stay at the Signum for ever, but she hadn't wanted to go just yet either. She had no doubt that Hamish would be able to cut off her funding, and maybe even have her thrown out. And it would all be so sordid. What with the divorce coming on with Owen. Alison was staring hard at her. Finally Sylvie smiled, a little fiercely, and raised her hand.

'Motion carried.'

They stood up and started gathering their papers. A few con-dolent hands fell on Hamish's shoulders. As she passed him, he said, though his words were barely audible, 'I do hope you know what this means.'

'I hope it means that the Signum will be a better place, Hamish, though it's beginning to seem as though it might have to become one without either your presence or mine.'

Alison grinned her way down the corridor.

'Coming for a drink at the Phil?'

'No, I don't think so. Better get back. Stuff to sort out.'

'All that shit with Owen, I suppose.'

'All that shit with Owen, yes. You put it so beautifully, Ali. See you next week.'

*

When houses closed around most places in Shropshire what you tended to find were a lot of dull, dead Victorian landscapes, incompetent watercolours of flowers, endless hatchet jobs in oils of sundry ancestors, the misshapen avatars from whom the inheritors had inherited. Once or twice Henry had been pleasantly surprised. But he tended to pick up what stuff he did buy from London or other dealers in Birmingham and Manchester. He knew what he wanted and they knew what he liked. He wasn't in any case one of those highly active dealers who was always hurtling about the place, but then neither were most other dealers. Not the ones Henry knew, anyway. They were a meditative lot – that's why they'd taken on the job in the first place.

But there were occasional surprises, and Henry had just had one. He'd been called to a house over towards Welshpool. An antique dealer who didn't want to get lumbered with too many paintings, particularly anything later than 1880, had asked him to come and sort out the pictures.

A large red-brick house. Its rooms were not so much filled as stuffed. Ragged bookshelves, ancient furniture, crooked pictures all over the walls. It had a curious atmosphere of dusty encroachment, the sense that time was beginning to scent a victory. It was all mostly indifferent stuff; Henry was about to say that he wasn't interested at all, when he spotted it in a corner. It wasn't even hanging on the wall, so it was a fair bet that no one had ever noticed its worth. It was a Ben Nicholson. 1930s. Henry had the eye, at least about things that interested him. He was hardly ever wrong. He looked it over and did a quick calculation. He remembered that the old lady had died. Everything was going to some distant relative, who probably had hardly seen her for the last few decades. No need for any great compunction then.

'I'll give you six hundred quid for the lot,' he said to the antique dealer.

'Make it six-fifty.'

'Split the difference.'

'Six-twenty-five.'

'When can you shift it?'

'Tomorrow. I'll get Martin to come over.'

'Done.' With that, the antique dealer was on his way. Henry waited until he could no longer be seen before going back upstairs and picking up the Nicholson. Might as well take it with him, but he didn't want anybody noticing. He wasn't sure, but thought he might be looking at the better part of £10,000.

Back in the gallery, he put the picture in a corner and stared at it. He poured himself a glass of red wine, then he thought he would phone Sylvie. He'd been meaning to do it. Now that he and Marie had discovered their compatibility, he wanted to let Sylvie know there were no hard feelings. It all made much more sense. Marie had had her children; she wouldn't be having any more. Henry had managed to avoid having any, what with one thing and another, and he suspected that now was probably not the time to start. But he had been aware that children would have to become an issue sooner or later with Sylvie. She had told him one night about the miscarriage, and then how she couldn't face all the treatment because of Owen's affairs, but at her age she surely wasn't just going to forget about it. In fact, had she let him get further than he did with his proposal that evening, then conception and motherhood would have been part of his proposition. Such an accommodating fellow, aren't I, Henry thought. But he hadn't got that far, had he? Just as well, perhaps. Or maybe he was rationalising again.

'Sylvie. Hello. It's Henry.'

'Henry.' He was genuinely pleased at the warmth with which

she said his name. 'Henry, how nice to hear your voice. I've been going to phone you. Can I come over and see you?'

'Well, yes,' he said. 'When?'

'How about now? The pizzas are on me.' Henry thought for a moment. Marie had gone to London for two days.

'All right. There's something I should say. I've met someone called Marie. Well, met her. I met her a long time ago. But . . . I can't offer you a bed for the night any more, Sylvie. It could be misconstrued by my new companion.'

'Well, I must say, you don't hang around, do you?' She had expected this remark to elicit laughter. It didn't. 'Sorry Henry, I was only trying to be provocative. Who is Marie?'

'She owns the Hilltop Gallery.'

'Then you have a lot in common. No, don't worry, I shan't need a bed. I'll forgo the wine, and drive back, but I'll bring a nice bottle for you, all the same.'

'Then I'll get the pizzas.'

Sylvie put her notebook in to her bag and threw on her leather jacket. She couldn't be bothered having a shower. She'd been making some decisions on the drive back over from Liverpool, and she did need to make her final notes on the *Vollard Suite*, but she wanted to see Henry too. It made it easier that he'd been the one to phone.

The music on Henry's CD-player wasn't Thelonius Monk, but Beethoven's *Opus 111*, his last sonata of all. Music seemed to confront silence here. If the two realms ever wanted to meet, whether it was the animal and the human or the angelic and the demonic, this would surely be their background track. It was music for the end of the world. Henry could never hear it without also hearing the river out there rising again. But now he let it play while he contemplated his new purpose and sipped his wine.

One of the other images of an artist on Henry's wall, apart from the photograph of Picasso with his *mirada fuerte*, was the woodcut of Beethoven that had embellished so many thousands of books. Batt had painted the composer in his middle years, almost bursting out of his skin with energy. Henry was greatly intrigued by this image and its implications. In it Ludwig is almost dementedly intense, surrounded by the debris of his life and trade: scattered coins, conversation-books in which visitors had to write their questions for a man who couldn't hear them, fragments of food, a candlestick, quill pens, a broken coffee cup. There is also the Graf piano, its strings looping out like springs from a burst mattress. He'd wrecked it trying to hear the sounds. What the woodcut didn't show was the chamberpot underneath the Graf, as reported by Baron de Trémont in 1809; the bowl containing the minotaur's faeces, but you can still smell them if you look hard enough and listen hard enough, the way Picasso said he wanted you to be able to smell the armpit of a woman once he'd painted her. Beethoven is oblivious to all the chaos that surrounds him, focused entirely on the string quartet he's now composing.

What was a sonata exactly? Henry had never entirely managed to work this out. He listened hard to this one as he stared equally hard at the Nicholson. It had to have a theme. The theme was then developed, which was another way of saying that the simplicity it craves is attacked by all the other musical possibilities surrounding it until it fights its way through. *En route*, by a process of osmosis, it absorbs much of the power of the surrounding forces until by the time it's finished, it's no longer the same as when it started. If the theme's not strong enough, the work fails. Sounds like all the rest of us there then, Henry thought to himself. He had to go outside, to make sure the river wasn't rising.

An hour later she was there. He offered her a glass of wine but she said no, she'd stick with water, having to drive back later. Then they went and sat in the Picasso Room. He'd already put the pizza in the oven.

'I'm glad about Marie,' she said. Henry shrugged. So was he, but he didn't necessarily assume it would all go on indefinitely. Take what comfort you can where you find it: that had become Henry's philosophy. 'And I'm glad there are no hard feelings.'

'Try not to go in for those any more. I'd better check that pizza.'

When Henry returned, Sylvie was taking notes with such concentration that he said nothing and went back for the salad. It struck him (unworthily?) that she might have wanted to see the *Vollard Suite* at least as much as she wanted to see him. Finally she seemed to have what she wanted and sat down to eat.

'So, what's happening with Owen?'

'He's moved out. We're getting divorced.'

'What will happen with the house? I thought you said you couldn't afford it without him.'

'I can't. I don't know, Henry. It's a very confusing time. And now there's a problem at the Signum too. This pizza's nice.'

'It's the one I give all my vegetarian ladies. That minotaur in the corner has started giving me a very old-fashioned look.'

'I suppose vegetarianism wouldn't be very good for business, if you were a minotaur.' They paused and ate until Sylvie spoke again.

'Thanks for everything, Henry. You were a real help sometimes.'

'Well, you got me through one or two dull evenings too.'

'Is that a new painting on the floor?'

'Early Ben Nicholson. It's been a good day.'

'Glad somebody's had one.'

When Sylvie arrived back in Chester later, there was a message for her on her answering machine. It was Patrick Gregory, wondering if he might possibly be able to speak to Mr Owen Treadle. The name meant nothing to her. She phoned him back.

'He doesn't actually live here any more. Is it about business?'

'It is about business, yes.' The voice was quiet and professional.

She gave him John Tamworth's number. 'You should be able to find him there.'

Ten minutes later John Tamworth picked up his phone and listened as the voice explained its identity, and the reason for wishing to speak to Mr Owen Treadle. Patrick didn't feel like any more subterfuge. He knew the newspaper piece would be coming out about the Delta Foundation the following Sunday. Now he just wanted to understand something, however fragmentary, about the way human beings behaved with one another. Particularly the ones who'd had dealings with his daughter.

'I can arrange the meeting,' John said. 'Would you mind it being filmed?'

'No. In fact I might prefer it. Is the filming for any particular purpose?'

'Not a specified one, yet. We're doing some work on memory and identity. Oh, there's one other thing.'

'What's that?'

'Mr Treadle won't know that you'll be coming. So I'll be introducing you in front of the camera.'

'Suits me.'

That night Henry had one of his most vivid dreams. The river was rising again. The river was always rising in Henry's dreams. The images had become so specific that Henry felt they could be filmed; now why was that? Was it because he spent his life staring at images, so that part of his brain had grown in power, the way one hemisphere of the human mind grew in size the more we'd used language? Who was he supposed to ask to find out? Sylvie certainly wouldn't know and Marie would merely laugh at him again.

'They have the new flood walls now, for heaven's sake.'

Walls against water. Might work for a while. In the dream they had a supply of sandbags. And Sylvie (what was she doing there?)

had acquired an information sheet which she placed before him. About all the infections flooding often brings in its wake. The pathogenic organisms one might cautiously expect. The nastiest type of flood water was apparently labelled Category C, which arrived after brownsludging it up from the sewers, sticky with unwanted matter from faeces and urine and the decomposing carcasses of drowned animals. Sylvie was weirdly detached as she explained to him the immemorial traditions of the deluge, and how industry had recently joined in with its own liberal sprinkling of lethal substances. Put all the hazards together and it appeared that everyone needed to be on the look-out for *E.coli*, particularly the sinister and apocalyptic strain known as 0157. Then there was salmonella, and the protozoa parasite cryptosporidium. There was also that age-old stand-by, cholera. Not forgetting Weil's disease. This apparently made its merry way through life by means of water contaminated by rats' piss, the Chardonnay of the damned. 'It's all one long litany of delight, isn't it, Henry?' Sylvie said, in a tone of insouciance which enraged him. He was locked in the immoveable paralysis of dream-rage. 'I daresay the minotaur's faeces are in there too. He's certainly roaring today, isn't he? Is that pizza ready yet?'

But dreaming Henry had no time for pizzas. He was already heaving the paintings upstairs, except that now he wasn't in Shropshire any more. He was in Florence in the middle of the 1960s. He stood above the Arno, for he seemed to be walking on water, and all around him he could see a town full of antique beauty drenched with the present's raging filth. He was shouting up to the Ponte Vecchio: It's going to take months, it might even be years, to scrape all the mire from those faces. Saints, madonnas, whores. And he knew with a thump in his heart that some of these things, things made through years of craft and devotion, would be lost for ever. So many things he loved.

Anyone peering across the river that night at 2 a.m. would have seen the figure of a small well-rounded man, his white pyjamas flapping in the breeze, peering down at the Severn as though he had dropped something, or someone, in it. Henry had awoken from his dream, and had gone out to reassure himself once more about the currents that raged around him.

Duet

Owen was out walking the walls. It was too early in the day for there to be many people out there yet. He liked it that way. As he walked he dodged the human vomit and the canine faeces, grateful only that it wasn't the other way around. Then he stopped opposite the warehouse and stared. He sometimes thought John imagined that shaping words into structures was easy. Because you didn't have to frame them and focus them, John seemed to think they were merely given. Perhaps they were; it wasn't as though Owen had ever made any up. He found them in dictionaries, in poems, on other people's lips. But he couldn't simply write them down like that, could he? He had to place them in their constellations, or they had no significance.

He hadn't been expecting this filming business, but he had started it off, hadn't he? And they had always had an agreement between them: wherever it takes us, that's where we go. It had usually been the other way around, with Owen pushing John further than he might have wanted to travel. Now their roles had been switched. He couldn't simply walk away, though that was very much what he would have preferred to do. He stared down at the canal. They had filmed its surface as though it were Deva, the mighty river, the local home of the goddess. It wasn't, of course, but the tight focus shot didn't let you know that. All it told you was that here was enough water for you to drown in. Enough mystery to make a play out of. He turned back. John had told him that today could be the last session with him sitting in front of the lens. He had also told him it might be a little different. Owen had a feeling that the change would not necessarily be a pleasant one.

When he arrived back he was surprised to see not one but two chairs set before the window.

'Someone else is joining us,' John said, fiddling with his camera. 'I'll introduce you when we start filming.'

Owen was already sitting in the chair when the doorbell rang. He had thought about it. It would be Sylvie, wouldn't it? His memory would be indicted for going absent without official leave by the person it had most affected over the years. But when John came back into the room it was with a man, someone Owen had never seen before. John took the visitor's coat and led him over to the other seat, and only when everything was in place, and the camera was once more running, did he speak to Owen.

'Owen, the man sitting next to you is . . . '

'I'd prefer to introduce myself, if you don't mind.' John nodded, to indicate he should go ahead. 'Mr Treadle, my name is Patrick Gregory.' He waited a moment for that news to sink in, then continued. 'Alex Gregory's father.' At this point Owen's eyes shifted from the man sitting beside him to John Tamworth's face. He had underestimated John. He'd always told Sylvie that his colleague's fatal weakness was a lack of ruthlessness at the sticking-point. If that had been true before, it didn't seem to be so any more.

Everything was in focus now. Anything once soft in outline had hardened. Patrick Gregory had opened the black notebook he was holding.

'Six months ago you made a film with my daughter, including a scene of such violence that she never got over it. This diary of hers makes it clear that this one scene changed her life for ever. Leading in fact to her death. I'd like to read you some of the extracts.' And Patrick started reading out Alex's words. He didn't need to date them, because the pattern they formed was an unmistakable one of trauma and retreat.

'I really wish I could talk to Isabelle Huppert about how she coped with the scene in Cimino's *Heaven's Gate* when the men rape her. How did she cope with that, the humiliation, her legs apart, blood all over her thighs? She looks terrified. But she fights back, and she must have known what was coming. I can't believe she didn't know what was coming. If I'd known what was coming I could have coped too, and in this film I didn't get to fight back. I only got to drown. Was it so important, Owen, to make sure you had my look of terror, fresh from the factory, to do that to me?'

Mr Gregory stopped then and stared at Owen, but Owen said nothing, so he started reading out the next passage.

'That time in Llandudno when we were filming *Time's Widow*, and you kept saying the take was no good, there wasn't enough grief in my face, then you finally set the shot up and walked across and whispered in my ear, "I'm leaving you, whether you're pregnant or not, pussy." That gave you a wrap, didn't it? What exactly do you think it gave me?

'You told me all I had to do was trust you. You said if I trusted you then everything would come out right. So I trusted you and everything came out wrong. I can't sleep at night without seeing those boys coming at me in those uniforms you put them in. I can see their eyes, feel their hands on my thighs. They weren't gentle hands, Owen. None of it was made any gentler because it was going down on film, you know. It was real. Was it worth it?'

Patrick Gregory read out the final passage he had chosen.

'I won't go to a psychiatrist. I don't believe in that type of medicine. People with their little rational machines poking about inside your head, inside your memory, trying to make adjustments to the mechanism. I've found a way out of this. I'm going away. When I come back I'll be free from everything that Owen Treadle and his world represent. When I come back I'll have the same look of serenity as Lady Pneuma. And for the same reason.'

He closed the book then, and John moved the camera slowly from his face to Owen's. If Owen had been an actor he could have been a good one, John thought, but he wasn't acting now.

'Don't you have anything to say to me?'

'Sorry. I'm sorry for everything.'

'That doesn't seem like enough.'

'I know.'

'There must be something else.'

Owen seemed to be finding it difficult to speak, something John Tamworth could never recall before.

'If she had died in war,' he said finally, 'and I had been her commanding officer, would you hold that against me?' The older man thought for a minute before speaking.

'Not if you had behaved responsibly in the battle. Not if you hadn't needlessly put your troops in harm's way.'

'Do you believe it's possible to make a film about war that's as serious as war is?'

'I'd have to think about that.'

'Well, I do. That's what I believe. That's my philosophy. It might be the wrong one, but it's mine. And if I couldn't make it real, then the film would have no value. I did what I thought was necessary to give those images reality.'

'You seem to have taken away my daughter's reality in the process.'

'She should have cared more about the outcome and less about the cost. When Visconti made *Death in Venice* he gave Dirk Bogarde some powder to put on his face that nearly took the flesh off . . . when Millais painted his Ophelia in the bath, Elizabeth Siddall nearly died of pneumonia . . . I didn't think she'd be so vulnerable. If I'd thought that, I'd have done it with someone else.'

'But you'd still have done it?'

'Yes. I would still have done it.'

Mr Gregory looked at Owen now with an air of professional scrutiny. He was in no doubt that the man was telling the truth, but he was not sure what the worth of this truth was; certainly not his daughter's life.

'It had better be good then, Mr Owen. This film that cost my daughter whatever tranquillity she'd managed to achieve in her mind. Is it possible to see it?'

Owen looked at John, and John looked uneasy as he closed down the camera, but he went across to his shelf and brought back the blank plastic case with the DVD inside it.

'This is an advance copy. The screening's still under discussion. There's some concern about the violence.'

'Can we watch it then?'

'Now?'

'You do have a DVD-player here, I assume.'

John pulled the curtains, having made them all a cup of coffee, and they sat down together to watch the film: the writer, the director, and the father of the young woman whose image had moved through the ravaged landscapes with the anguish of Cassandra, or sometimes the mute stoicism of the young woman in Bresson's *Balthasar*. There was a lot more voice-over than dialogue. Owen had been assiduous. There were quotations from Herodotus and Caesar, the *Anglo-Saxon Chronicles*, Hitler, Churchill, Wilfred Owen, Tony Harrison. And each set of words was accompanied by the same ragged bunch of anonymous soldiers, fighting, killing, being killed, looting, raping. The mystery at the heart of this mystery play was how we could continue to do this to one another, after thousands of years of seeing the consequences. They moved across a devastated landscape, something like the paintings Paul Nash made of the trenches. The music thoughout was taken from one or another of Bach's cello suites, and the unavoidable plangency of that sound combined with the images was irrefutably moving. And then towards the end a new set of characters turned up for the torture and the female booty. What had happened was that Alex had grown so used to the boys doing the acting with her that she no longer looked afraid. She knew them too well to have the genuine look of fear that Owen wanted. They had all enacted so many horrors together that horror had been temporarily transcended. They had become too comfortable in their images of one another. So he'd had an idea: they'd set the scene up, and then at the last minute he'd put the boys from the street in. He made the other actors give him the costumes back and told them to take the night off. He'd picked some local rabble, hanging about out there.

'What do we have to do?'

'Put some funny clothes on and act nasty.'

'We do that anyway.'

'I'll pay you for it.'

'How much?'

'Fifty pounds each.'

'Where and when?'

That's what had happened. But even Owen had been astounded at their feral menace as they swooped around, and then descended on, Alex. He was hidden just off camera, and he could tell as she clutched his hand that this was genuine terror. Which had been what he had wanted, wasn't it? It wasn't as though he was glorifying war or rape, after all. The image of the horror had to be real to warn against the reality of the actual horror. To confront the mystery, the horror of the passion, day after day.

In the film, when they'd done with her, they threw her body into the river. Which was the canal standing in for Deva, the war goddess who presided over the slaughter and the subjugation. The body wrapped in dirty garments floated on the surface. And the final scenes showed the Dee Estuary, the delta where the river met the sea and the waves ran one into another. The saddest of the cello suites played as the image faded out.

John pulled the curtains back as the credits scrolled. Mr Gregory watched carefully to see that his daughter's name was properly credited. It was. He had investigated rape cases, and he tried to view these scenes with the same objectivity that he'd listened to the evidence years before. But he couldn't. He had seen the terror in his daughter's eyes. There was no faking that. Mr Gregory now stood up. He turned to look at Owen.

'If it had been pornography, I would have done everything in my power to destroy you. But it isn't. I can't doubt your seriousness of purpose, even if I can only lament your methods. I hope you don't seduce all your young actresses. Could I have a copy of the film, please?'

John looked uneasy at this.

'Technically, it hasn't been released. I mean, it's not yet in the public domain. It will be screened by the BBC at some point, but there might have to be alterations.' Patrick Gregory simply looked at him in silence until John gave in; he walked over to the DVD-player, took the disc out, put it back in its box, and handed it over. Patrick now turned back to Owen.

'Did Alex ever speak to you about Lady Pneuma?' Owen started laughing, if a little bleakly, then stopped himself.

'Yes. Living on air, wasn't it? Alex was into so many cultish notions, I could hardly keep up.'

'That's why she went to Scotland. To put that particular belief into practice. To rid herself of the stains of the flesh. She seemed to think the biggest stain of all was you, and this.' He held up the DVD. 'Look in the Sunday papers this week. You'll find quite a lot about Lady Pneuma. Don't think they'll ever find any other young ladies starving themselves to death up in that bothie.'

At the door, Mr Gregory finally turned to John.

'It does seem to me, Mr Tamworth, that you must share equal

blame with Mr Treadle, just as you share equal credits for the film. You could have switched your camera off at any time. You could have asked the young men to leave. And if I got it right, Mr Treadle was hidden under the pile of rags, so he couldn't actually see the look of terror on my daughter's face. You could though, couldn't you, as you looked through your lens? Caught up in the excitement, were you? Realised just how strong the footage would be? It wouldn't surprise me if you two weren't in for an award or two for this one.'

Then he was gone.

The Tragic Lecture

Fatum. Sylvie's mother had once explained the word to her. It was related to karma, but not the same thing. *Fatum*: it's the one bit inside you that won't be told. The part that's once bitten twice bitten, once shy twice shy. The ineradicable, the unreformable, the incorrigible splinter of your soul that even Orpheus with his lyre or Saint Michael with a hymning throng of angels could not beguile to be anything other than precisely what it is. It's what you're stuck with, brother. No one and no thing can talk it out of being irreducibly thus in all its bloody-minded authenticity. *Fatum*: it'll get you into trouble. It'll lose you friends. It'll go down into the grave at last, but not before you do. Even a century of therapy or sympathetic magic can never coax it out of you. *Fatum*: it's there to stay. It can even get you married. It had certainly got Sylvie married.

If you believe in it, then you also had to believe that external events connived to fashion it thus and thus. Otherwise it couldn't have its potency, could it? The phone call had come half an hour before. Alison.

'Don't get me wrong, Sylvie. I'm not trying to get rid of you or anything. But the job could have been described with you in mind. History of images. Photographic, artistic, cinematic. The iconography of perception. A particular interest in the popular arts and music would help. That's you. It's your subject, your articles, your book.'

Sylvie had taken the computer reference and downloaded the

application form. And it was true. The post of Senior Lecturer in *Images, Their Function and History* seemed to have been customised to fit her work and her obsessions. She had printed out her CV: she could update that quickly, and complete the application. Given the time of year of the advertisement, it was evidently a rush job. Something had fallen through, or someone had pulled out. This made it all simpler. If she had somewhere else to go, then the rest fell into place. She would resign from the Signum, and sell the house. Then she would bugger off, without a single tear shed for anything or anybody. Except maybe Henry and his minotaurs. Alex Gregory might have died but she had still been the other woman in her marriage. She couldn't actually weep for her.

Sylvie had been right. It was a rush job. The course had almost been cancelled because a new vice-chancellor wasn't keen on it, but there had been too many applicants, since it had already been advertised in the prospectus. Even better: the course leader knew of Sylvie's work and admired it. She was asked to wait behind after her interview. Five minutes later, Bernard Stanley walked towards her smiling.

'Do you want to come to my room, Sylvie?' Once inside he turned round from his desk without sitting down, and said, 'We're in a position to offer you the post if you could commit yourself now to taking it.'

'I'll take it.'

'You're absolutely sure?'

'No question. I understand the teaching you want done and I understand the terms. But I can be quite confident there'll be no change of heart on your part?'

'Quite confident. Let's go back and talk to the dean then, shall we?'

So Sylvie was now preparing her last lecture of the year for the Signum with a mood not far off gaiety. After she had delivered it, she would go and deliver her resignation to Hamish Flyte, who she had heard might not be around to receive many more of them. The last thing the university needed at the moment was an affiliated institute so disaffected that half its members of staff hated the Director of Studies. They were about to give him the old heave-ho, but dressing it up with the usual palaver about early retirement, enhanced pensions for distinguished service, and what-have-you.

She walked out past the *For Sale* sign, and got into her car. Owen's was there gathering dust. Why had he suddenly stopped driving? Then off she went, down the usual roads, through the usual traffic, until she began the big concrete dip that ended in the tunnel. All that water thrashing about above her. She'd taken the ferry over once, to see what it was like sitting on top of the water instead of being underneath it. She remembered those dreadful dreams of Henry's. Always the Severn rising and flooding his beloved gallery, soaking his pictures, drowning the poor mino-taurs. You could hear their bellows up above the waves, and you could hear Henry's bellows tangled in the sheets. For some reason she suddenly remembered Alberto. He'd been around years before Owen turned up. She had met him in Italy and they had had one of those holiday affairs in which everything seems wonderful. He'd spoken barely a word of English. By the time he turned up the following year to re-claim her, he'd learnt a great deal more. The more English he learnt, the more she disliked him. It was as though his personality couldn't survive the translation. He did have a beguiling line in curses, all the same. His speciality was a series of remarkably inventive imprecations involving the penetration of a fellow's mother's orifices by the fellow himself, with the clear implication that, while all this oedipal thrusting and seeding was going on, the very last thing in the old dear's mind would have been to remark, 'Now just cut that out, you little motherfucker.'

She sat on the table. She was wearing a short black dress and black tights. Tights though, not stockings. She was happy to give Lionel his last glimpse of her thighs, but didn't want him catching the white of her flesh. She wanted him to take something away from the lecture apart from another heavy dose of sexual frustration. She switched on the overhead projector and slid the image over the glass.

'Minotaur: the early Christians tried to turn him into an image of the devil, with Theseus as the Christ-figure who kills him. But that wouldn't do. That simplified life far too much. Look at this bull-man, roaring at the centre of his mystery, sweating hair and blood. The pagans might have had a better idea with their: *regressus ad uterum.*

'Now it's worth making a note here that Ovid describes this creature as *semibovemque virum, semivirumque bovem.* Which is to say, half-bull-man half-man-bull, and which isn't to say that a man's head sat upon a bull's shoulders; that is very much by way of subsequent interpretration.

'Picasso would never relinquish this beast, our therianthrope. He sits in the centre of his iconography, although it must be said that this cave is often a cave of flesh. His darkness, his rage, the endless stinging rebuke of his desire, these remained Picasso's themes throughout his life. And his blinding, which appeared largely to be his own addition to the mythic iconography. The beast blinded, led away by a young girl with a candle.

'Now look at this image from the caves at Lascaux. I want you to look at it hard, while I put some ideas before you. Our fate as a species is to reside in consciousness, but this is a tragic fate. It means that wherever we are, we're also elsewhere. This is at the root of that famous lament of Keats': 'O for a life of sensation, rather than of thought.' And as far as we can see this was our fate from the very beginning. Deep down in those caves in Lascaux, Chauvet or Altamira, we can be pretty sure of one thing: there were no aurochs or bison down there, only their images. Now whether our ancestors from the Upper Palaeolithic were in shamanistic trances or not, they had taken away the image from the point of its perception. They drew the image without the creature before them. Once we have separated the image from the point of its perception, we have started to carry the world around inside us. And it's grown heavier and heavier. The more lenses we fill our world with, the more images there are to carry. Down in the caves, they had only two.' Sylvie pointed to her eyes. 'But how many have we got?

'Imagine if you were far enough away, high above New York, the way the lens was so far away from the Large Magellanic Cloud. If we had sensitive enough equipment up there we could see the extraordinary geometry of the city's streets; there's a labyrinth if ever there was one. And then a tiny flash of light, which will travel on through the darkness at 186,000 miles per second, and then another flash and another. It's going to travel for 160,000 light years, so whole epochs will pass before what has happened here happens there. Our Magellanic observers then see a moment in history. Tiny flashes in the labyrinth. John Lennon has been shot over and over again in the back. He stumbles and the spectators move forward. Their eyes are filled with that dazed wonder, just like these children in the *Vollard Suite*.'

Sylvie now removed her final image from the glass.

'Lenses and constellations. Try to be aware of them. This is how we construct reality.

'And just before you go, I'd like to thank you all for your attention. Because this is the last lecture I'll be giving at the Signum Institute. I'm leaving to go elsewhere.'

The murmur of complaint that went across the lecture hall

gratified her. Lionel came up to her as she was gathering up her notes.

'Are you really going?'

'Afraid so, Lionel.' He stared at her beseechingly. Oh God Lionel, she thought but didn't say, there must be some female undergraduate here prepared to take you to bed, even if she does have to dry your head out first. Then she went and delivered her letter to Hamish. It had given her a certain amount of pleasure to tell the students before him.

'It's not open to negotiation, but then I gather you won't be in any position to be doing much negotiating from now on, anyway.'

She left then. She had one more place to go before packing up her things and preparing for Kent. She walked down the road steadily in the direction of the Physics Department. She only knocked once on the door and walked straight in. Helsey had a female student with him.

'Ask her to leave. Ask her to leave and come back later.'

'Annette, would you mind coming back in an hour or so.'

'I have a lecture.'

'Then make it tomorrow.' The student stood up and collected her essay, with evident bad grace. She gave Sylvie one final stare and left the room. Attractive girl though. Wonder how many personal tutorials she gets each semester.

'That wasn't very nice, what you did,' Sylvie said, before the door had closed. She had forgotten how attractive he was. The tall forehead, the high cheek-bones.

'I'm sorry. Sorry for everything.'

'And the letter to Hamish fucking Flyte saying I seduced you. Are you sorry for that? That let you hang on to your professorship, did it?' He looked genuinely startled.

'I never wrote a letter to Flyte. He wrote one to me.'

'I saw the letter, Tom. Don't lie.'

'You can't have seen the letter, because I never wrote one.' She stopped and thought back. Actually, she hadn't seen any letter, had she? Hamish had only let her catch a glimpse of the letter-head, then he had ordered her out of his room, after giving her a version of what he said were its contents. Tom was rustling through one of his drawers. He pulled out a sheet of paper.

'This was the only communication that passed between us.' He handed her the sheet. It was from Hamish to Tom. She read:

Dear Dr Helsey,

I am aware of the recent goings-on in this building involving yourself and a member of the staff here.

I have heard through the grapevine that you are up for a professor-ship. There has also been some gossip about your behaviour with a number of your female undergraduates.

If it were to come to the attention of the authorities that you deliberately set about getting a member of my staff drunk, then bringing her back to these premises to have sex with her, I don't think your prospects would look very good.

I would be obliged if you did not return to the Signum for some time. I also think it would be wise of you not to attempt to contact Sylvie Ashton again.

Should you do so, I might feel obliged to take further action.

Yours sincerely,

HAMISH FLYTE
Director of Studies, The Signum Institute

Sylvie read it twice.

'I want a copy.'

'That's the only reason I didn't answer your calls.'

'I want a copy.'

'What are you going to do with it?'

'Never you mind, Tom. I want a copy. Photocopy it for me.'

He did as she said. He went to the end of the corridor, and photocopied the document.

'Do you want me to do some copying for you, Professor Helsey?' the secretary called from her office. Nothing out in the corridor ever escaped her notice.

'No thank you, Jean. It's just the one sheet.'

Then he walked back to his room and handed it over.

'Looks like it's goodbye, then. I'm leaving the Signum.'

'I'm sorry.'

'Oh do stop saying you're sorry, for God's sake. Let's find something positive to say to one another, since we'll probably never be speaking again.'

'It was a beautiful evening,' he said, with evident sincerity, and held out his hand.

'Yes, I didn't think you were a bad fuck either, Tom.' With that she kissed him on the cheek, very gently, and left.

Rising Waters

Bernard Trasker MBE was back in the gallery, minus his wife. He was looking at the Nolan *Rimbaud* with intense interest. Finally, he emerged from his own reverie, stared at his watch and then shook it. It had stopped. He looked around him from wall to wall. Henry watched him from his seat behind the desk, and smiled. He spoke now, but only to himself.

Ah, I see you've finally noticed the clock, Bernard. Or rather its absence. There are no clocks in casinos; no calendars in hell. This isn't a casino, of course, and it certainly isn't hell – it's Shropshire, and really rather pleasant, but time still bends here all the same. If you ever go to Ramsgate you can still see the clock down by the harbour giving the local hour, permanently at variance with Greenwich Mean Time. I'm told in all French stations before the Great War each clock would give *l'heure de la gare*, five minutes slower than the time in Paris, and in those days to cross the US, you had to keep adjusting your watch every time you crossed the line. Here too in the Riverside Gallery the clock hands turn to a tempo of their own devising. Which is to say that they don't turn. Henry wouldn't have clocks in the gallery, and had no watch of his own. This, he felt, disadvantaged him not at all.

Time though. You certainly couldn't escape it by exiling the faces of clocks. He had been making a few mental notes while looking at a new book on the *Vollard Suite*: Rembrandt in Picasso's portrayal had become a mountain of fleshly curlicues, the ludicrous meanderings of elderly troubles and senescence.

Thus did Picasso anticipate his own decline. Thus did he point out in visual terms that time only gains its contours by passing you through its valley of shadows. The more decrepit Rembrandt becomes in the etchings the more firm-limbed and perfectly-contoured are the young women he gazes upon. Rembrandt is now a confusion of lines; old age a scrollwork of over-fussed confusion. Youth is clean, clear and fecund, but is that only in the eye of the artist? Is it a reality, this cleanliness, this clearness, or a creative achievement? Is it ever possible to make the distinction in any case? Henry had no idea.

'I'm going to buy it.'

'Quite sure, Bernard?'

'Quite sure.'

'I'll wrap it in brown paper before delivering it to your home.'

'I want to take it with me now. I've got the car outside.'

Bernard made out his cheque, for a substantial amount, but Henry found it hard to believe it wouldn't be honoured. In any case he knew where the man lived. And they took it out together. Put it on the back seat.

'A glass of wine, Bernard?'

'I won't actually.'

So Henry was left alone in his gallery, with a gap on the wall he'd have to think about filling. The payment meant he didn't have to worry about a number of things he probably wouldn't have worried about very systematically anyway. But the know-ledge that he wasn't worrying about them would have worried him. In one sense he was sad to see the Nolan go. It was such a dry, scorched, arid painting. Rimbaud having the sockets of his heart and mind burnt out. It had seemed to him like a talisman against floods and drowning. Something so dry even the Severn could never come near it. He could not understand why he had become so obsessed by the notion that the things he most loved would be taken away in the waters. He knew it wasn't logical, but then how much of life ever was?

Henry opened one of his better bottles to celebrate. He stood at the edge of the gallery's garden and stared at the Severn.

'Why, do I know you are going to take something away from me? You or one of your sisters?'

He woke at three that morning, shouting, choking, fighting away the sheets that were sheets of water, coughing the sludge out of his lungs.

'It's all right, love. All your minotaurs are safe and so are you.' Marie's arms were around him, gently caressing.

'I'm going to move them all to the top floor tomorrow,' he said. 'Or I'll never get another decent night's sleep.'

The Shipwreck of the Singular

Summer turned to autumn and then winter. The chronicle of events, as ever, unfolded. The revelation of Lady Pneuma's eating habits, and some of her other habits too, sexual and financial, destroyed the Delta Foundation. She didn't go to prison, all the same, even though some like Patrick Gregory felt that she certainly should have done. The last he heard of her she was starting up a public relations company in Wisconsin under another name, and he had a queasy feeling it would be a great success. She had re-married, apparently. Her new husband was very old, and very rich.

Deva appeared finally, with no cuts, at ten o'clock in the evening on BBC4. It was acclaimed. It was finally given two prizes, one for the script and one for the direction. John Tamworth and Owen Treadle were reconciled, if they'd ever in truth been unreconciled. And they had a new production on their hands, *Claparède's Drawing Pin*. 'Ground-breaking' it was being called. Owen now lived in a flat in the same block as John, having agreed with Sylvie what proceeds should come to him from her house, which had been sold for a substantial price. Henry Allardyce had moved all his Picassos up to the top room of the Riverside Gallery, where he sat every evening, staring at them and then down at the river. He was glad of the space he had placed between the minotaurs and the water. He had also met all of Marie's children, and had almost brought himself to be civil to her elder son, whose self-important financial wizardry represented everything he most detested in life.

At least the bumptious young fellow wouldn't be needing to borrow money from them.

And as for Sylvie, she had sold up for more than she expected, settled matters with Owen, and moved to Whitstable, where she now had a four-storey Edwardian house looking out over the sea. It was within twenty minutes drive of the university. There the students seemed to like her, and she liked them, so far. If there was a Hamish about, she had not yet encountered him. Hamish had already left the Institute, but not before Sylvie had phoned him a number of times.

'I have an interesting document here, my friend. It's a letter from you to Dr Tom Helsey, who I gather is now Professor Helsey.' She then read him the text of the letter. There was a silence she greatly enjoyed. 'I gather you have been pensioned off with all sorts of enhancements, Hamish. I can't help thinking that if this piece of paper comes to light, your pension might get de-enhanced.' She'd kept the line alive long enough to hear his deep breathing, then she'd rung off. She'd performed variations on this routine for several weeks, until she'd grown bored. Let the bastard crawl off into a corner and die.

Ex-Detective-Inspector Patrick Gregory had watched *Deva* more times than he could recall, despite the pain it undoubtedly caused him. He could never see the rape scene without feeling momentarily nauseous, without foreseeing his daughter's death in a ramshackle hut on the west coast of Scotland.

'I only hope you realise how good you were, my love. That takes acting beyond acting. They've even given you a posthumous award, but that's not going to bring you back.'

As the autumn term finished, Sylvie decided that she needed a break, a serious break. There was money in the bank, the divorce proceedings were almost complete, and for the first time she could remember she felt easy about her work and her life. She thought of Owen and Chester and the Signum Institute, and it all seemed like another life, an alien life she'd been redeemed from. A labyrinth she'd finally escaped.

And that's why she bought the last-minute airline ticket to Bangkok, at a price so low it made her laugh. Thailand, where she had been once before, many years before, but she could still remember the astounding politeness of the men, the agile beauty of the women, the blazing colours of their clothes; the glorious beaches. Ah yes, those glorious yellow beaches.

She'd had an affair. Was that the right word for it? Can an affair only last a fortnight? Sexual relationship sounded so clinical. How many years ago was it now? Ten, twelve? One of the smiling young men had come up to her and introduced himself. Exquisitely mannered as he was, he had peered with undisguised curiosity at the flesh her bikini left uncovered. They had slept together in her little rented hut that night. His first blonde western woman; so she reckoned anyway, despite his insouciance about it all. It struck her as pretty likely that another like him might come along now. She deserved him, after all, what with Owen, Tom Helsey and all the rest of it. Even though her body had spread a little here and there – outgrowths of flesh, simultaneously soporific and wayward. She had stayed home and worked for the last five months. But she had eaten too. And had the odd bottle of wine. No matter. Once he was into the softest part of her, she would make him happy, whoever *he* was. And he wouldn't notice in the dark, not once she got going. She might give the bikini a miss though, just for the moment. Keep herself tantalisingly covered in white and blue muslin. She looked in the mirror. She didn't have anything to worry about yet, except possibly impregnation, by the wrong party at the wrong time. But then all that needed seeing to anyway, didn't it? So it didn't seem very likely, just at the moment. God, when was she going to sort all that out? Not now, that was for sure. Might be some serious work needed there. Poking around inside her with their pincers and blades. But not now. Not now.

She arrived safely enough, but God she was tired. Something about flying, speeding you up and wearing you down at the same time. Was it the cosmic rays at great heights – didn't they move through you with unexpected rapidity, leaving you seriously sieved-out and wonky? Owen had had some sort of theory about it, which he'd often treated her to, but then Owen had had theories about lots of things.

She was on the beach called Khao Lak, gazing at her book of images when the noise finally reached her. The birds had fallen silent hours before, dogs had all set off inland, quietly, their tails twitching down like dowsing sticks, but no one had noticed this on December 26th 2004. Now the tsunami was hurtling towards her at five hundred miles an hour. She looked up and saw how the ocean had risen to its full height and started running. It was arriving back in a terrible hurry to swallow the earth once more. In the last few seconds she had time to stand, register the panic of all those around her, turn and start to make her escape along with the rest of them, but she travelled no more than a few feet before the deluge covered her, sweeping her along in its raging current. Her lungs were filling with salt and water. She was soon unconscious. One of the thousands of bodies swirled about with all the cars, wooden houses and telegraph poles; the desks, chairs, bicycles and beds; the swollen bodies, both large and small, before the sea surged back out once more, most of its human inventory still undeposited on earth. So many bodies moving with the currents somewhere, rising and falling.

Coda

You can't grieve for a void. That's why weeping relatives on the news ask for the bodies back, so they might be properly buried and mourned. That's why widows travel half-way round the world to see where their soldier husbands fell in battle. Even a little urn filled with ashes will suffice. Something to put down in the earth, somewhere to cut words in stone. And that was why Sylvie's mother wept each day on the phone to Owen when he called her. He even drove over to see her, though they had never much liked one another.

'She must be dead, mustn't she? She would have contacted us by now.' At sixty-five, Sylvie's mother had dyed her hair orange. This, it seemed to Owen, made her look even madder than she had before. She had always alarmed him. Hardly surprising Sylvie's father had divorced her.

'She must be dead, my little Sylvie. It's been four weeks. I managed to get through to the British Embassy over there, but they didn't seem to know any more than we do. She's dead, Owen. She is, you know. My daughter's dead.' She wept, and Owen found himself on the verge of tears too. Sylvie had already exited his life, but he really hadn't wanted her to leave everyone else's too. Not like this.

So they'd buried her already in their minds. Poor Sylvie. Then they had to get their mental shovels out and dig her up again. Despite the battering she received from the flood, Sylvie survived.

She realised who she was again one day in a shanty hospital, hastily constructed, ten miles inland from the coast. She was surrounded by human wreckage of one sort or another, and found it very hard to walk at first. When a British official finally turned up weeks later, she had the greatest difficulty speaking to him. She was flown back to England. A visiting lecturer had been given her courses to teach, using some of the notes which Sylvie herself had posted on the university's website, but she assured the dean that she would be giving her own courses again very shortly, even if she could only keep herself upright with the help of a walking-stick. She had already managed to start driving again, which was how she had arrived at the Riverside Gallery. She'd quelled her mother's wailing finally, and the day before she'd had her reunion with Owen and John. So now she had come over to see Henry, without telling him of her visit beforehand. It was a very rainy day and she could no longer distinguish the rain from his tears as he stood out in the drive with his arms about her; he had seen her through the window making her difficult way down the drive and had run out to meet her.

He held her by the shoulders and looked at the marks on her face. She would never look quite the same again, that was for sure. The ravine across her forehead mapped out the point where she had collided with something very hard, with all the force of the tsunami behind her. He led her under the awning, out of the rain, and pulled her towards him as they stood in silence for what might have been minutes. Sylvie had no idea; she had lost all sense of time.

'You really did get a battering, didn't you? It must have been terrible.'

'Don't remember anything about it, Henry, to be honest. It's as though it all happened to someone else, someone who was travelling under my name at the time. For weeks I remembered nothing. I just lay there and hurt. Then bits of me started to come back. But not the tsunami. That's never come back. Maybe it was too big to remember. No space inside large enough to contain it. If I could only find a photograph of myself being swelp along in the water . . . You always had the right idea, watching out for the flood, but you were looking in the wrong direction, my love.'

'Knew it was going to take something precious from me. Always knew that. Strange, isn't it? Didn't expect it to ever bring it back though.' He kissed her, very gently, on her bruised and cratered cheek. 'Can you really remember nothing about it?'

'Nothing. I've started looking through photographs. As if, if I could see the pictures of it, I might meet myself coming the other way. Can you understand that?'

'Yes. I think I can. Something to do with the persistence of vision?'

'What isn't?'

Then the children started filing out of the bus and down the drive. Sylvie looked at Henry, and Henry smiled, almost apologetically.

'It's the talk I do for Shropshire schools, remember. On Picasso. Today's the day.'

'Mind if I stay and listen?' Henry shook his head.

So Sylvie sat on the chair he provided for her as Henry did his usual number. It was all carried off with good humour and a deft lightness of touch, but he couldn't disguise the formidable knowledge that lay beneath it, as he spoke of Ambroise Vollard and Picasso. He went through the etchings and engravings one by one, pointing to details and encouraging the children to think about why the artist had made the choices he had. He explained to them that they themselves were the young people staring at the minotaur, and that the minotaur took many forms. Some of them might be destined to become minotaurs one day. In which case, they'd find that they were both hunters and hunted.

'We live inside this dark place, all of us, and the future is only ever an inch away. The future is all those people approaching with lights. So where do we find the strength to step out into the future? By swallowing the past: that's the secret. You mustn't ever let the past swallow you. You can check this with your biology teacher when you get back, but I think you'll find that time swallowed turns to energy inside you. Digest it slowly, then let it transmute inside your intestines. Your acids can dissolve it, don't ever doubt that, even a rhinoceros skin properly cooked will go down through the heart of you and come out; it might even come out as one of these images. That's what he did, you know. That's why we're still looking at all these pictures you see about you. He swallowed the past and never let the past swallow him. That's the one thing everyone in this room can learn.

'So, let's try to imagine, shall we, on this very wet Shropshire day, what it might have meant to be Pablo Picasso. If only for that single moment of recalling how we once saw a minotaur, chased a unicorn, ate a lion, and swam with sharks. Look carefully at the pictures hung up on the walls around you and see if you might hear a distant roar still fading away.'

Two months later Henry Allardyce stared at the Severn in the darkness and wondered when it would rise again. Walls wouldn't keep it in for ever, he was sure enough of that. He drained his wine-glass and then turned from the river, back to the house where the lights were going out one by one. Soon enough Marie would be between the sheets and he'd be beside her. And when he woke at three or four in the morning, drowning in the invisible tide, she would hold him close and tell him not to worry. Tell him to stop thrashing about. There's nothing to worry about, Henry, she'd say. We're nice and warm here. And dry as a bone.